Maybe Image really was bad luck. . . .

"Try to move your arm."

Supporting her elbow with her right hand, Melanie rotated her left shoulder. "It's okay. Just banged up." Tears came into her eyes. "Don't worry," she said quickly when Christina furrowed her brow. "I'm not crying because of my shoulder. It's Image. I can't believe she acted so crazy. She was doing so well!"

Christina smiled cheerfully. "Don't be so hard on yourself. That spreader would have spooked any horse."

"It's not just that, Chris." Melanie shook her head, flooded with doubt. "Whenever I start feeling confident about Image and her training, something like this happens. What if Fredericka had been here? What if she'd seen me get dumped?" Melanie swallowed a sob of misery. "That would have been it for us. Maybe everybody's right. Maybe Image *is* bad luck, and I'm just wasting my time!"

Collect all the books in the Thoroughbred series

THOROUGHBRED Super Editions
Ashleigh's Christmas Miracle
Ashleigh's Diary
Ashleigh's Hope
Samantha's Journey

ASHLEIGH'S Thoroughbred Collection
Star of Shadowbrook Farm
The Forgotten Filly
Battlecry Forever!

* coming soon

THOROUGHBRED

PERFECT IMAGE

CREATED BY
JOANNA CAMPBELL

WRITTEN BY
ALICE LEONHARDT

HarperEntertainment
An Imprint of HarperCollins*Publishers*

HarperEntertainment

An Imprint of HarperCollins*Publishers*
10 East 53rd Street, New York, NY 10022

Produced by 17th Street Productions,
an Alloy Online, Inc. company

HarperCollins books are available at special quantity discounts for bulk
purchases for sales promotions, premiums, or fund-raising.
For information please call or write:
Special Markets Department, HarperCollins Publishers,
10 East 53rd Street, New York, NY 10022.
Telephone: (212) 207-7528. Fax: (212) 207-7222.

ISBN 0-06-105854-8

HarperCollins®, 📖 ®, and HarperEntertainment™
are trademarks of HarperCollins Publishers

Cover art © 2000 by 17th Street Productions,
an Alloy Online, Inc., company

First printing: December 2000

Printed in the United States of America

Visit HarperEntertainment on the World Wide Web at
www.harpercollins.com

❖ 10 9 8 7 6 5 4 3 2

"I'LL ONLY BE A MINUTE, PROMISE," MELANIE GRAHAM SAID to her friend Kevin McLean as she opened the door of his pickup truck. Kevin had parked beside the gates that led into the backside of the Keeneland racetrack.

"A minute?" Kevin laughed. "I doubt that." Turning off the motor, he slid down in the driver's seat and pulled the brim of his baseball cap over his eyes. "Wake me when you get back."

Rolling her eyes, Melanie hopped from the truck and shut the door. Kevin was probably right, she thought as she hurried across the asphalt. She would be more than a minute. But not *much* more. Vince Jones had ordered her to stay away from his stable area, so she would have to make her visit with Image brief.

It was eight o'clock on a Tuesday night, and the

1

backside was empty except for a few workers. Tall lights illuminated the area, casting eerie shadows over the rows of barns. Nervous, Melanie jumped at every sound. She hated sneaking around like this to see Image, but she had to.

Not seeing her beloved filly wasn't an option. Ever since Image had been whisked away from Tall Oaks, Fredericka Graber's farm, to the track, Melanie had missed her desperately. This would be the first time Melanie had seen Image since the horse had been at Keeneland. It had been only five days, but as far as Melanie was concerned, five days was way too long.

With Kevin's help, Melanie had worked with Image at Tall Oaks every day for the last three weeks of summer. They had made terrific progress, and Melanie's dream of being the first to ride Image was about to come true when Vince suddenly ordered the filly back to Turfway Park, where his other horses were racing at the time. Melanie knew the filly wasn't ready for the track, but in his eagerness to get the two-year-old ready to race, the stubborn trainer had ignored her protests.

Vince doesn't understand, Melanie thought. She had worked hard to gain the filly's trust. Slowly that trust had turned into a special bond. But that was hard to explain to an old-fashioned trainer such as Vince. To him, Image was just another Thoroughbred.

As she hurried past the track kitchen, Melanie

glanced around nervously. If Vince caught her, he'd be so furious he'd probably tell security not to let her on the track. On Monday, when the trainer had moved Image from Turfway Park to the Keeneland track, he'd made it clear that Melanie was not welcome at Keeneland, either.

Which isn't fair, Melanie said to herself. Okay, so maybe it had been stupid of her to tell Vince Jones— the premier trainer on the East Coast—that he didn't know how to handle Image. Image wasn't even Melanie's horse. But couldn't Vince see *her* side?

Obviously not, Melanie thought as she made her way toward Vince's barn. Vince Jones would never admit that he didn't know how to handle Image, even though the disastrous weeks at Turfway had proven it. The feisty, strong-willed filly had broken away from her handlers and trampled her grooms. No one could get close enough to Image to come anywhere near riding her. But not only had Vince refused to listen to Melanie's advice, he'd finally gotten sick of Melanie's arguing and interfering. That was when he'd told her she couldn't see the filly anymore.

When she reached Barn 15, Melanie stopped by the side of the building and took a deep breath. She knew there would be at least one groom on duty. Thoroughbreds were too valuable not to have someone watching them every minute in case one got colic, or cast in its stall, or went off its feed. Melanie could only hope that

3

the worker would be sitting in the barn office or, even better, off at the track kitchen getting a snack.

Peering around the side of the building, Melanie could see the office door, which was halfway closed. She didn't see anyone inside, but when she listened carefully, she heard voices. Maybe the groom had a friend visiting, or was talking on the phone. Either way, Melanie was pretty sure she could get to Image's stall without any problem.

As she jogged down the row of stalls, the horses snorted and started. A few hung their heads over their stall guards, hoping for attention. Since it was the beginning of October and the nights were cool, most of the horses wore light blankets.

"Sorry, guys, can't visit," Melanie whispered as she hurried past. When she reached Image's stall, she took one last look around before unlatching the top door. Unlike the other horses, who had nylon stall guards or wire mesh half doors, Image's stall had a bottom door of solid wood and a top door of steel wire mesh. The filly had proven to be an escape artist; the only way to keep her in was to put her in this jail cell of a stall.

"It's me, pretty girl," Melanie murmured as she swung open the top door. Immediately Image popped her head over the lower door. Her brown eyes were huge, her nostrils flared. Throwing up her head, she sucked in the night air, then let out a plaintive whinny.

4

"Shh." Melanie put a finger to her lips. The filly stared into the night, a half-wild look on her face.

"Oh, Image." Melanie ran her hand down the filly's neck. "What's happened to you?"

A pang of sadness filled Melanie. She knew Image hated to be closed up in a stall. At Tall Oaks the filly had been turned out night and day in her own pasture. Since Image had been back at the track, the luster had gone out of her black coat and the curious gleam had dimmed in her eyes. But Melanie thought that Image seemed even worse now. Her wide eyes were frantic; her neck was crusted with sweat.

"Hey, I brought you a treat." Melanie pulled a carrot from her back pocket. Image swung her head around so fast she knocked the carrot from Melanie's hand. When Melanie bent to pick it up, the filly threw herself against the bottom door, hitting it so hard it sounded like a thunderclap.

Melanie put a soothing hand on the filly's neck, but Image bobbed her head, spun, then lunged at the door again. Tears sprang into Melanie's eyes.

Quickly she opened the bottom door and slipped in, latching it before Image hit it again. For a second Image stood quietly as she studied Melanie. "It's me," Melanie whispered, holding out the carrot again.

Image lipped it from her palm, then banged the bottom door with a front hoof. Melanie scratched under the filly's forelock, trying to distract her. Blinking back tears, she glanced around the stall. The filly had pawed her bedding down to the dirt floor in many places. There were fresh marks on the walls where she had scraped her teeth. And though the stall was clean, bedding and hay were heaped into messy piles, as though the groom had left the stall in a hurry.

All were signs that Image was miserable.

The filly had lost weight since Melanie saw her last, and her coat was dry and flaky. None of the grooms liked working her, which meant that no one took the time to really care for her.

"Oh, Image." Melanie let out a sigh. "How can I help you?"

Talk to Fredericka, Melanie thought, answering her own question. Image's owner, Fredericka Graber, loved the filly, too. She had to be aware that something was terribly wrong with her horse.

Melanie *had* already told Fredericka several times that Vince had moved the filly from Tall Oaks too soon. But just like everybody else, Fredericka felt that the veteran trainer knew best.

Melanie fed Image another carrot. "This time I'll convince Fredericka that you need to go home," she added emphatically. "I promise."

Twirling in the stall, Image pawed frantically, then stuck her head out over the bottom door and whinnied. Several horses whinnied back. As much as Melanie hated to go, she knew it would be only a matter of time before a groom came around to find out what was agitating the horses.

"I'll try to come back tomorrow," Melanie said. Kissing the filly's nose, she opened the door, barely squeezing through before the filly rushed for the opening—and freedom. Hurriedly Melanie slammed and latched the bottom door. Her hand hesitated on the top door. Although she hated to do it, she knew she had to shut the filly in. The last time Image had escaped had been a disaster. She'd raced onto the track during the workouts and collided with Gratis, one of the colts Vince Jones was training. Gratis had needed stitches, and her cousin, Christina, who had been riding Gratis at the time, had sprained her wrist.

A second mishap would be a catastrophe for Image. Fredericka was already worried that Image was too spoiled and unruly ever to make it as a racehorse, and Melanie knew that Brad Townsend had been pressuring her to sell the filly to him for breeding.

Melanie shut and latched the top door, wrinkling her nose distastefully at the thought of Brad getting his hands on Image. Brad Townsend would never tolerate the filly's behavior long enough even to try to train her to race. Image had great bloodlines, though, and Brad wouldn't let that go to waste. Image would be sway-

7

backed and fat before her third birthday. Only Melanie believed that the filly had the heart, power, and conformation to be a champion racehorse. Too bad no one would listen to her.

Sighing with frustration, she hurried back to the parking lot. When she reached the pickup, Kevin was snoring softly. At first Melanie thought he was acting, but when she shut the door of the truck, he jumped in his seat, banging his head on the ceiling. His baseball cap fell onto his lap, and he looked at her with glazed eyes. "Did you make a goal?" he asked.

"Uh, no," Melanie said, biting back a laugh. "Are you all right?" She touched Kevin's arm, and he smiled sheepishly.

"I must have been dreaming. I thought I was in the middle of a soccer game." Smoothing back his red hair, he replaced his cap. "How long were you gone?"

"Only a few minutes," Melanie fibbed.

He checked his watch. "More like half an hour."

"Obviously you needed the nap. Too many late-night dates with *Lindsey?*" she teased. Melanie and Kevin used to date, but they had broken up at the beginning of the summer after they decided they were better off as friends. At first Melanie had been jealous of Kevin's relationship with Lindsey, another senior at Henry Clay High School, but she soon realized that he and Lindsey were perfect for each other. As long as

Kevin was still her friend, she was happy for him.

"No, too much homework and soccer," Kevin grumbled. "I'm glad we have the next three days off for fall break. I need a rest. So how was Image?" he added as he started the truck.

"Not good," Melanie answered, her brow creased with worry. "I need to talk to Fredericka. She has to know that Image hates it here."

Kevin glanced over at her. "I'm sure she does. But she also trusts Vince. He's been the farm's trainer for as long as I can remember, and you know Kentucky horse people and tradition."

"Yeah, yeah. And I'm just a girl and I'm still only a bug—so what do I know?" Melanie grumbled.

Kevin chuckled. "You got it."

Melanie sat bolt upright in the seat and crossed her arms stubbornly. "But I *do* know. I know Image better than anyone!"

"You don't have to convince me."

"Does that mean you'll drive me to Tall Oaks now, so I can talk to Fredericka?" Melanie asked hopefully.

"Sure. There's no school tomorrow, and Lindsey's out of town with her folks, so I'm free to drive you."

"Thanks." Melanie settled back in the seat. Keeneland racetrack was only six miles from Lexington, so it wouldn't take long to get to Fredericka's farm. "Where'd Lindsey's family go?"

9

"They have a cabin on a lake. She invited me to go with them, but with the soccer playoffs next week, the coach wants me to keep working out." He patted his knee. "It's almost back to normal."

Kevin had hurt his knee in another disastrous incident with Image. During one of her training sessions, the filly had knocked Kevin into a post, and he'd slammed his leg against it. A hematoma had developed in his knee, which had taken weeks to heal.

Glancing out the window, Melanie chewed her lip as she thought about what she could say to Fredericka that she hadn't already said. But all Fredericka had to do was look at Image to know that Vince's training plan wasn't working.

When they pulled up in front of the Civil War–era mansion, Melanie hopped out. "Will you come in with me?" she asked Kevin. "After all, you've been a big part of Image's training, too."

"I will—but this is your battle, Mel," Kevin reminded her. "You have to make your own case."

"Fair enough."

Fredericka's maid answered the door on the first ring. "We heard the car drive up," Luanne said in her southern drawl. "We wondered who was visiting this late." She led the pair into the sitting room. Fredericka was sitting in a high-backed chair, reading. Although it was late, she was dressed formally in a tailored skirt and long-sleeved silk blouse. Her gray-streaked hair was pulled back in a silver clip.

When Fredericka's husband, Charles Graber, had died, his wife had taken over the running of the horse farm. She'd expanded the number of stallions, added a stallion barn, and hired a new farm manager. Her most successful colt, Gratis, also trained by Vince Jones, was currently racing at Belmont, the prestigious track in New York.

"Ms. Melanie Graham and Mr. Kevin McLean," Luanne announced. Fredericka put her book aside and stood up.

"What an unexpected pleasure," she said, smiling sincerely. "Is everything all right, Melanie?"

Melanie cleared her throat. Fredericka had been polite and gracious throughout her ordeal with Vince. She had to choose her words carefully. "I wanted to talk to you about Image."

Still smiling, Fredericka nodded. "Now why am I not surprised? Luanne, would you please bring us some lemonade?"

"That's okay, we're only staying a minute," Melanie said quickly. She glanced at Kevin, who stood framed in the arched doorway, his baseball cap in his hands. He was looking around the room. A fire crackled in the brick fireplace, warming the high-ceilinged room. Buckles and buttons in display boxes were arranged on one wall, swords and pistols

11

hung on another wall, and a rifle stretched across the mantel.

"My husband's Civil War collection," Fredericka said, noticing Kevin's interest.

"Fredericka, I went to see Image tonight," Melanie broke in. "She looks *terrible*. She's thin and dirty. Her stall's a mess, and she's so miserable she's chewing the walls. I can't stand to see her locked in that . . . that *cell*."

"I know, dear."

"You know?"

Fredericka nodded. "Of course. Vince keeps me informed—he's very aware of Image's condition—and I visit her often."

"Then why aren't you doing something about it?"

"I am. I'm listening to Vince's suggestions. He's trying a new supplement to help calm her, and blinkers to help her focus."

Melanie's eyes widened in disbelief. "He's *drugging* her?"

Tilting her chin, Fredericka gave Melanie a look of displeasure. Melanie flushed. "I'm sorry. I didn't mean it to sound like that. I'm just worried about Image, and I don't think supplements and gadgets are going to help."

"What do you suggest?"

Melanie was so surprised that someone had asked her opinion, she was momentarily speechless. "Uh, well, I—I think Image needs to come back to Tall Oaks," she finally stammered. "She needs to learn to race *here*, where she's relaxed and comfortable. Then she needs to train at Whitebrook, or a similar farm with a large training track, where she can gradually get used to other horses and a starting gate and the noises at the track. Then maybe she can go back to Keeneland. But most of all, she needs to work with *me*."

By the time Melanie was finished, tears blurred her vision. Fredericka was sitting back in her chair, studying her intently.

"Well, you've obviously put a lot of thought into this, dear," Fredericka said. "But the person you'll have to speak to—and convince—is Vince. He's been the farm's trainer for more than twenty years. Charles trusted him, and so do I. I'm not about to fire him, Melanie."

Melanie winced. "Vince? But he won't listen. He doesn't even want me around his barn."

Fredericka's gaze didn't waver. "Then you've got your work cut out for you."

Shoulders slumping, Melanie looked at Kevin for help. He shrugged. "Mrs. Graber's right. Vince is the horse's trainer. It's him you need to talk to."

"B-But . . . I—I . . . ," Melanie stammered.

Standing, Fredericka walked over and gave Melanie a little hug. When she pulled away, she was smiling. "Vince isn't the enemy, Melanie. He wants Image to succeed, too. And he's trying. You just have to approach him the right way."

"You mean I can't call him a lousy trainer and a jerk?" Melanie muttered as she wiped her eyes.

Fredericka laughed. "Right."

Melanie inhaled deeply, as if to regain her strength, and then blew her breath out. "Okay. I'll talk to Vince first thing tomorrow morning." It wasn't going to be easy, Melanie knew. But she also realized she had no choice. "I just hope he'll listen."

At six o'clock in the morning Melanie found Vince at Keeneland's training track. The trainer was huddled in a windbreaker, watching the morning works. The sky was gloomy with clouds, and a fine mist floated in the air. As Melanie approached him she shivered, more from nervousness than from the fall chill.

Her footsteps crunched on the gravel path. "What do *you* want?" Vince demanded gruffly, stopping Melanie in her tracks. He hadn't even turned his head. How had he known who it was?

"Uh, I spoke with Fredericka last night, and she suggested I talk to you," Melanie said, shoving her hands in her jacket pockets. A horse galloped past, mud flying, and Vince wrote something down on a clipboard.

14

When he didn't say anything in response, Melanie went on. *After all,* she thought, *I've got nothing to lose.*

"I . . . I wanted to ask once more if you'll let me work with Image," she said hesitantly. All night long she'd practiced what she would say to Vince, vowing not to sound too negative. "I really miss her, and I think she misses me."

Tilting his head, Vince cocked one bushy brow. "What makes you think that?"

"Uh . . ." Melanie thought fast. She didn't want him to know that she'd been visiting the filly. "Well, we got pretty close before you moved her to the track, so I just figured she missed me."

With a snort, Vince turned his attention back to his clipboard. "You sound like your cousin, Christina, when she talks about Star. Not many people in this business would nurse a half-dead colt back to health if they knew he would never race again."

"Christina would *never* give up on Star," Melanie declared. "She loves Star, just like I—" Quickly she caught herself before her voice rose in anger. She knew Vince wouldn't listen if she argued with him. He was used to giving orders and having them followed.

"I mean, I am like Christina in that Image is special to me," Melanie began again. "I'd like another chance to work with her—and you," she added. "I promise I'll follow your rules."

15

Throwing back his head, Vince let out a hearty chuckle. "You? Follow rules? That'll be the day."

Melanie smiled weakly. She should have known Vince wouldn't be interested.

"Well, thank you for listening." Eyes downcast, Melanie quickly turned to go. Her bottom lip was starting to quiver, and she didn't want him to see how upset she was.

"You'll have to start at the bottom."

Melanie stopped in her tracks. "Pardon?"

"As a groom. That's the only way I'll take you on."

Melanie's heart leaped into her throat.

"I know you're in school," Vince continued, "but I expect you to be here every minute you're not." His gaze was hard and challenging as he waited for her reply. Melanie understood what he was saying: If she wanted to work with Image, she'd have to give up everything else.

Since she'd come to Kentucky, she had been working hard to lose her bug—her status as an apprentice jockey—and become a winning professional jockey, riding as many horses for as many trainers as she could. But Melanie didn't hesitate to tell Vince that she'd groom for him.

Nothing was more important than Image.

2

"YOU DID *WHAT*?" CHRISTINA REESE EXCLAIMED. SHE WAS kneeling in the straw, a bottle of liniment in one hand. She'd been rubbing Wonder's Star's legs, trying to keep his ankles from stocking up.

"I told Vince Jones I'd groom for him," Melanie repeated. After Kevin had dropped her off at White-brook, she'd gone straight to Star's stall, knowing that her cousin would be there.

Standing up slowly, Christina stared at her cousin with an expression of disbelief. "Mel, I know you love Image, but do you realize what Vince is asking?"

"Of course," Melanie said impatiently. "He expects me to start at the bottom, mucking stalls, cooling horses, cleaning tack—"

"It means you won't have time to exercise-ride at

Whitebrook *or* at the track," Christina interrupted. "And you won't be able to race."

Melanie slapped herself on the forehead. "Oh, I hadn't thought of that," she joked.

Christina gave her head a quick shake. "Okay. It's your life." Turning, she screwed the top back onto the liniment bottle and stuck it in the grooming box.

Frowning, Melanie leaned against the door frame of the stall. "I thought you, of all people, would understand." She pointed to Star, who stood listlessly in the middle of the thick straw. The two-year-old colt looked worse than Image. He'd been sick with an unknown virus and had lost so much weight that his ribs stuck out. "You've done *nothing* but nurse Star for two weeks."

"That's not true. I've kept up with the morning works," Christina replied, defending herself.

"But you haven't ridden in any races, *and* you gave up your chance to ride Gratis for Vince at Belmont in a race that could have put you on the cover of every racing magazine," Melanie continued to argue. "Admit it—you've sacrificed a lot to be with Star. Can't you see why I want to do this for Image?"

Christina furrowed her brow. Reaching up, she ran her hand down Star's neck. His once glossy chestnut coat looked muddy brown, and his muscles were so weak that when he moved, his hind legs wobbled.

Early that morning the veterinarian, Dr. Stevens, had assured everyone that the worst was over, but he still couldn't predict if the colt would recover totally. "It's different, Melanie," Christina finally said. "Star's my horse. You don't own Image."

Melanie felt as if she'd been punched in the stomach. She opened her mouth for a snappy retort, but nothing came out. Christina was right. Melanie had no control over what happened to Image. And as a jockey, she would be foolish to get so attached to a filly she couldn't even race yet.

"What if you give up everything and Fredericka still decides to sell her?" Christina continued. "Or Vince doesn't let you ride her? Remember, you'll be working for him as a groom—not a jockey." Christina gave Melanie a searching look. "And isn't that what you really want? To ride Image? To race her one day?"

"Well, yes," Melanie said. "But I'm only going to groom for a little while—until I prove to Vince that I'm the right person to train and ride Image. Right now I just want to make sure she gets the love and care she needs. You should see her, Chris. She's skinny and miserable. If I don't do something, she'll be ruined forever. She'll never even make it to the track."

"But Mel, what if—"

Melanie raised her hand to stop her cousin's question. "I know what you're going to ask: What if I work with Image and she's still too crazy to race? I don't know, but I think she deserves a fair chance. And if I fail"—she grinned at her cousin—"I'll still love her, just like you love Star."

Christina grinned back. "You're even more hopeless than I am, Mel," she said, shaking her head.

"No way!" Melanie answered with a laugh.

"So, when do you start as Vince's groom?" Christina asked.

"First thing tomorrow morning."

"Need some tips?" Biting back a smile, Christina held up the grooming box. "It's been a while since you lowered yourself to picking out hooves and mucking stalls."

"That is *so* not true. I used to brush Image every day," Melanie retorted, though she knew her cousin was teasing. "But I do have one problem—how am I going to tell your mom I'm not exercise-riding the next couple of weeks?"

"Since Mom's been working with the yearlings, Cindy's been scheduling morning works. You'll have to talk to her about it. I think she and Ian are still in the office. I'll walk over with you." Pulling a carrot from her pocket, Christina offered it to Star. The colt's ears pricked forward, but then he turned his head away.

"Oh, Star," Christina said, her voice so filled with sadness that Melanie put her arm around her cousin's shoulders.

"He'll get better, Chris," she said. "It's going to take a while, that's all."

Christina nodded. "I know. I just hate to see him like this. It's like he's a totally different horse."

"I know what you mean," Melanie said, thinking about how much Imago had changed since the summer. "Believe me, I know."

Melanie helped Christina blanket Star and wrap his legs. After saying goodbye to the colt, they headed to the office in Whitebrook's training barn. Although the virus Star had picked up at Belmont had not been identified, it was thought to be deadly, so Star was stabled away from any of the other horses, in quarantine.

Deep in their own thoughts, the two girls walked across the stable area. The fall air was crisp, and Melanie hugged herself to ward off the chill.

Compared to most Kentucky Thoroughbred farms, Whitebrook wasn't huge. But the three barns, training track, and spacious paddocks were beautifully maintained. Christina's parents, Ashleigh Griffen and Mike Reese, and the farm's other employees worked hard to make sure that Whitebrook lived up to its reputation as a top-notch training and breeding facility.

Melanie had been living at Whitebrook for four years, but she never grew tired of the farm's beauty. She especially loved it at this time of day, after the morning works, when everything was peaceful. Inside the barns, the stallions, broodmares, and horses in training contentedly munched hay, and outside in the pastures, the mares and weanlings grazed on sweet Kentucky bluegrass.

As the two girls approached the training barn, a determined voice broke the silence. "No, you may *not* make an appointment for me. I'm not having any operation." The voice came clearly from the open window of the farm's office.

Melanie stopped outside the barn door and glanced at Christina. Pausing, her cousin put a finger to her lips. "Cindy," Christina mouthed. Cindy McLean was the adopted daughter of Kevin's parents—Ian McLean, who was Whitebrook's head trainer, and his wife Beth. Cindy was a jockey, too, but she'd come home several weeks ago after Belmont's track doctor had ordered her to take time off from racing.

"You think your shoulder is going to heal all by itself?" Ian answered his daughter in an exasperated tone.

"No. But if I have the operation, Dr. Singh said, it might be a month before I could use my arm and a *year* before I could ride again," Cindy continued, her voice rising. "At least now I can use it, and maybe after a couple more weeks of rest, I'll be able to start exercise-riding—"

"Cindy, you're fooling yourself," Ian interrupted. "A torn rotator cuff is not going to get better without an operation. You've been nursing that shoulder for years. It's time you did something about it."

"But a *month*, Dad. What am I supposed to do with myself?" Cindy sounded as if she were on the verge of tears. "What if I can't ride as well ever again? My whole life is racing horses!"

Instead of embracing her time at Whitebrook as a well-earned vacation from the track, Cindy had been depressed and miserable. Then she had gotten involved with the work at the farm, and her mood had improved slightly. She was helping to nurse Star while Christina was at school, and she had taken over the morning works. Still, hanging out at White-brook was kind of a comedown after years of racing winning Thoroughbreds on some of the finest tracks in the world. Melanie could see why Cindy was frustrated.

"I know it will be hard," Ian said. "But remember, your mom and I will support you. Just like we've supported you in everything you've wanted to do—even when it meant you were traveling all over the world. And you haven't been the best at writing or calling, you know."

Melanie heard Cindy groan, then say something Melanie couldn't make out. Melanie glanced guiltily at Christina. She didn't want to eavesdrop, but she had to talk to Cindy. Christina looked just as uncertain about what to do. They stood in the open doorway of the training barn, hoping no one would see them.

Then Melanie had an idea. She leaned her weight against the big barn door and slid it halfway closed, making sure to rattle it loudly. Christina rolled her eyes and stifled a giggle.

"Hey, Cindy! Are you still here?" Melanie called down the aisle. Several horses whinnied, as if hoping that it was dinnertime already.

"In the office!" Ian called back.

"Act like we didn't hear them," Melanie whispered to Christina as they walked down the aisle. When Melanie and Christina entered the office, father and daughter were busily going over a racing program for the upcoming weekend. Ian was propped on the top of the desk, and Cindy was seated in the swivel chair.

"Hi!" Melanie greeted them a little too loudly. "I'm glad you're still around, Cindy. I wanted to tell you that I'm not going to be able to ride in the morning works for a while."

Cindy had cropped blond hair, and her face was sun-weathered. Though she had the demeanor of a teenager, dressed in old jeans, a Whitebrook T-shirt, and sneakers, her face was creased with worry. For a moment she stared at Melanie as if she didn't know what the younger girl was talking about.

"Oh, yes. The morning works," Cindy said finally.

"That's all right. Naomi's brother, Nathan, is back from Florida, so he can ride. Christina, you can gallop the horses that need prerace prep, and Dani can handle the ones that just need a light workout."

"Dani's exercise-riding?" Christina asked. Dani was one of Whitebrook's grooms.

"She was doing such a great job ponying, we started her trotting some of the horses coming off layups," Cindy explained.

"We needed her," Ian added. "Christina, you've been busy nursing Star, Kevin can't ride because of his knee, and Melanie, you've been off with Image."

Cindy looked at Melanie. "Is that why you aren't going to be working horses for us?"

"Yeah. Vince Jones wants me to help him in the mornings."

"That's great," Cindy said, sounding wistful. "I raced a few horses for Vince last winter in Florida. He'll be able to teach you a lot about riding and *winning*."

Christina gave Melanie a curious look. Melanie shrugged. Okay, so Cindy thought she was *riding* for Vince, not grooming, but that wasn't Melanie's fault.

Besides, Melanie thought excitedly, *just wait until I convince Vince that I'm exactly the right person to work with Image—as a groom, and eventually as her jockey.*

• • •

25

"Your first job is to take these to the laundry," said Julio, Vince's barn manager, pointing to a mountain of horse blankets piled in the corner of the tack room.

"But I didn't get to say good morning to Image!" Melanie protested. It was five-thirty Thursday morning. Joe Kisner, one of Whitebrook's workers, had been able to give Melanie a ride to Keeneland. Whitebrook had several horses stabled at the track, and Joe was responsible for them in the mornings.

Julio snorted. "No time for that kind of foolishness. You're not a jockey anymore."

"What's that supposed to mean?" Melanie asked.

"It means you follow orders." Picking up the blankets, he plopped them into Melanie's arms. They were so heavy, she stumbled backward.

"Where is the laundry?"

"You'll figure it out," Julio called as he headed out the door. Melanie wrinkled her nose. The blankets were damp with urine and manure, and when she tried to get a better hold on them, the buckles on the straps banged her in the knee.

She gritted her teeth. She'd known before she started that the stable workers would give her a hard time. Not only was she the new kid, but she was a jockey. Some jockeys treated stable workers like dirt, which meant there was no love lost between them. But Melanie knew she could handle it. Some of the more experienced jockeys gave the apprentice jockeys a hard time, and Melanie had learned to deal with them.

"Okay, I can do laundry," Melanie muttered. "But *first* I'm going to see Image."

Still carrying the blankets, she staggered out the door and down the covered aisle in front of the stalls. Horses shied, and a guy yelled at her to get out of his way. Ignoring him, Melanie dropped the blankets beside Image's stall. She peered through the wire mesh of the top door. Image was standing in the corner of the stall, her butt to Melanie.

"Hey, princess," Melanie crooned. "It's me. I'm here, just like I promised. How about a bath?"

"Graham!"

Melanie turned to see who was blasting out her name. S.J., one of the other workers, was coming toward her with a huge wheelbarrow. The sun was just rising behind the rows of barns and the vapor lights were still on, but the backside was bustling.

"You've got stalls one through ten," S.J. said, parking the wheelbarrow in front of her.

S.J. was Melanie's age, but he'd dropped out of high school to work full time. He had long, scraggly hair, he wore a baseball cap backward, and his cheek bulged with chewing tobacco.

"A wheelbarrow?" Melanie stared at him in disbelief. "Don't you have something a little more modern—like a tractor and a manure spreader?"

"Got something even better." Grinning, he held up a pitchfork. "Just dump the manure in the bins over there." He pointed to the end of the barn. "The manure guys haul it away in their dump trucks."

Melanie peered toward the end of the barn, then back at the wheelbarrow and pitchfork. She groaned. It would take forever to clean ten stalls. "Okay, but first I've got to take the blankets to the—" she started to explain, but S.J. was striding across the drive to the other shed row, whistling happily, as if cleaning ten stalls was his idea of a great time.

Melanie blew out a breath. When she turned around, Image's black head was still in the corner of her stall. Unlatching the doors, she went inside. The filly hadn't touched her bucket of grain. Scooping up a handful, Melanie sniffed. It smelled funny. She bet Vince had added the calming supplements.

"I wouldn't eat it, either," Melanie muttered. Quietly she walked toward Image's head and scratched under her mane. Pinning her ears, the filly moved away. Melanie dropped her hand, saddened by Image's sullen behavior. It was as though she didn't even know who Melanie was. "I've got to get Vince to let me work with you again," she said determinedly. "Before it's too late."

Then Melanie remembered what she'd promised Vince—she had to follow his rules. Sighing with frustration, she gave Image a hug. She'd just have to work extra hard to get her chores done so that she could spend as much time with Image as possible. The filly needed her, and Melanie wasn't going to let her down.

3

THE LAUNDRY ROOM WAS CROWDED WITH PEOPLE WASHING and drying rags, towels, bandages, and blankets. Melanie dropped the pile of dirty blankets on a huge table. As she stuffed the oversized washing machines with the smelly blankets, she listened in on one of the conversations.

"Hey, I've got a great tip for you," a young girl was saying to her friend. She was stocky and wore a yellow knit shirt with the name of the farm she worked for over the pocket. Melanie glanced over her shoulder to see if she could read the name, but the girl was too far away. "Put this week's paycheck on Celtic Mist to win. He's racing Saturday in the Blue Blood Stakes."

Melanie pricked up her ears. Celtic Mist was Brad Townsend's new colt. He'd arrived from California only a week before, so Melanie was surprised to learn that Brad was running the two-year-old so soon.

"Yeah, I heard his works this morning were awesome," the other girl said. She was bent over, pulling towels from the dryer. "Whatever happened to the Townsends' other colt, Wonder's Star?" she asked, straightening. She was taller and wore the same yellow shirt.

"He disappeared. I heard he has some horrible disease." Shrugging, the smaller girl picked up a pile of newly rolled leg wraps. "If you ask me, that Christina Reese got what she deserves. She was always bragging about how wonderful the colt was—telling everybody he was the next Derby winner."

Melanie could feel the heat rise into her cheeks. Whirling, she faced the two girls. "If you don't know what you're talking about, you should keep your big mouths shut."

For a second the two girls seemed startled. Then the taller girl put one hand on her hip and gave her a smug look. "What's it to you, anyway?" she challenged.

"Christina doesn't brag. And Star may have been sick, but he's getting better, and he still might win the Derby."

"How do you know? Are you Reese's valet or something?"

"No, I'm her cousin—and I'm not a valet, I'm a jockey."

The shorter girl gave Melanie the once-over, then said, "Sure, you're a jockey. That's why you're doing laundry with the rest of us."

At that, the taller girl snickered. Picking up their piles of clean towels, the two girls left the laundry room, still laughing.

"Oh, who cares what they think," Melanie grumbled as she finished filling the washing machine. Track gossip could be vicious, and it spread like wildfire. Anyone working on the track had to learn to ignore it.

After setting the cycle and water temperature on the washers, she hurried back to the barn to start mucking stalls. When she arrived, she saw Billy and Marianne, two of Vince's regular grooms, going into Image's stall. Marianne was carrying a saddle. Billy had a twitch in his hand.

Melanie's stomach lurched. A twitch was a metal-handled gadget with a loop of rope at one end. The rope was tightened around the upper lip of a horse. Distracted by the pain, the horse was supposed to submit and stand still.

It looked as though they were going to use the twitch to saddle Image. Melanie couldn't believe it. And she couldn't just stand by and let it happen.

Furious, she charged into the stall. Image was

backed into a corner, Marianne holding the lead hooked to her halter. The filly's head was high, and her eyes rolled as Billy approached her with the twitch.

"What are you doing?" Melanie demanded.

"Saddling this nutso horse," the groom said, his back to Melanie.

"With a twitch? But that's so cruel . . . and it's *not* necessary!"

"It is if we don't want to get killed," Marianne said, her eyes not leaving Image. The filly was sitting back on her haunches, as if ready to bolt. She was trembling from head to tail, and her ears were pressed flat back.

Rushing forward, Melanie put her hand on Billy's arm. "Please don't twitch her. I'll saddle her. I've saddled her lots of times."

Dropping his arm, Billy gave her a doubtful look.

"Hey, why not let her?" Marianne said. Stepping away from Image, she handed the lead to Melanie. Billy shrugged and nodded at the old exercise saddle propped against the wall. "It's all yours." Then he strode quickly away, as if he was relieved not to have to deal with Image.

When Billy left, Marianne said apologetically, "It's not that we wanted to twitch her. It's just that we didn't want to get hurt. Yesterday she struck at Julio and almost took his arm off. Vince was furious. He said we had to get the saddle on her today and he didn't care how we did it. This morning all the grooms drew straws to see who had to work with her. Billy and I lost."

"I understand," Melanie replied, her heart still pounding with emotion. "But I think I can do it if you leave me alone with her for a while," she said quietly. Marianne nodded. When she left, Melanie pressed her lips together, trying not to cry. Image turned away and stuck her head in the corner.

Melanie took a deep breath. Obviously all the grooms hated working with the filly. If Melanie could prove she was willing and able, they'd gladly let her do *everything*.

Holding out her hand, Melanie slowly walked toward Image's head. Then she stopped. She was still holding the lead. She didn't think the filly would bolt for the partially open door, but she couldn't be sure. Image was a master at getting away; once she'd dragged Melanie across the pasture. However, if Melanie closed the door and Image went ballistic, she might get trapped and maybe trampled.

Melanie caught herself. What was she thinking? This was the horse she loved, not a wild bronc.

Image had one ear cocked, as if wondering what Melanie was up to, but when Melanie took a step forward, Image pinned both her ears threateningly. Melanie halted in her tracks, suddenly realizing that

Image *wasn't* the same horse she had loved. The last few weeks had changed her. Melanie had lost the filly's trust—the trust she had worked so hard to gain. Now Image didn't even seem to know who Melanie was anymore.

A familiar voice coming from outside made Melanie look out the stall door.

Instantly she realized who the voice belonged to— Brad Townsend. He was the last person she wanted to see.

Melanie pulled the bottom stall door shut, then reached for the top door, but it was too late. Brad had spotted her. When Melanie saw that he was walking with Fredericka, her pulse quickened.

Was Brad again putting pressure on Fredericka to sell Image? Image was the daughter of Townsend Mistress, who had been one of Brad's mares. When Mistress lost her first foal, Brad had figured she would be worthless as a broodmare and sold her to the Grabers for a huge amount of money. Kevin had told Melanie the whole story—how Brad had bragged about the deal. But when Mistress had gone on to have four beautiful foals, the Grabers had had the last laugh. Now Brad wanted Image so that he could breed her and carry on the Townsend Mistress line. And Melanie knew that when Brad Townsend wanted something, he'd do just about anything to get it.

"Melanie? What are you doing here?" Brad asked in his usual imperious tone. He was dressed in creased navy pants and a sport coat. Even at the track, he looked as if he were at a fancy cocktail party.

"Working," Melanie said, noticing for the first time that Alexis, Fredericka's farm manager, was standing slightly behind Brad. Melanie narrowed her eyes as she looked at Alexis. It was the first time she'd seen the farm manager since Vince had taken Image from Tall Oaks. Melanie had no proof, but she was convinced that Alexis had something to do with Image's hasty departure from Tall Oaks. Alexis had never hidden her dislike of the feisty filly. What was she doing tagging along with Brad at the track?

Fredericka smiled. "Congratulations on your new job, dear!"

Brad frowned in confusion. "What do you mean, congratulations?"

It was none of Brad's business, so Melanie chose not to answer him.

"She's working for Vince Jones now," Fredericka explained. "That way she can continue to work with Image. How is my baby, Melanie?"

"Not happy." Melanie stepped aside. She wanted to tell Fredericka about the other grooms using the twitch, but decided against it. She was working for Vince now. If he knew she was running to Fredericka with every complaint, he would fire her on the spot.

"Hello, sweet girl," Fredericka crooned. When she heard Fredericka's voice, Image swiveled her head around. "Princess, I brought you a treat." Fredericka held out a piece of carrot.

Image pricked her ears, but then she turned away, her head hanging low in the dark corner. Fredericka's smile faded. "You're right, Melanie. She has gotten worse. I'm glad Vince hired you—you can keep an eye on her."

"Vince hired Melanie to train Image?" Brad asked, looking completely bewildered. He crossed his arms over his chest and glanced from Melanie to Fredericka, as if demanding an answer.

"No, he hired me as a groom," Melanie said. "But I'm hoping to work with Image, if Mr. Jones will let me."

Brad shook his head. "That's crazy. I'd better have a word with Vince. He has to know he's wasting his time." He pointed his finger at Image. "That filly is too spoiled ever to be a racehorse, Fredericka. She just doesn't have what it takes."

"I have to agree with Mr. Townsend," Alexis said. "I know how much you love Image, Fredericka. Can't you see she's miserable here?" With a sympathetic expression, Alexis touched Fredericka's arm, and shivers ran down Melanie's spine. Alexis didn't care about Image—she was such a faker!

"Listen to Alexis, Fredericka," Brad pressed. "And ask yourself how much money you're going to throw away on this filly before you realize that she'd be much better off eating grass and raising foals at Townsend Acres."

A pained expression crossed Fredericka's face. Melanie knew that money was a big issue with Fredericka. The older woman was working hard to make Tall Oaks a successful Thoroughbred farm. Since her husband died, Fredericka had spent a lot of money updating the farm's facilities, hiring Alexis, and buying horses. Several times she had hinted to Melanie that it was more expensive than she'd anticipated, which was the only reason she was even considering selling Image to Brad.

Composing her face, Fredericka faced the two. "Brad, you have been a friend of mine for many years. Alexis, you are an excellent manager and helped me buy my wonderful colt, Gratis. I thank you both for your advice; however, I will decide what's right for Image."

Brad nodded politely, and Alexis smiled as if conceding to Fredericka, but Melanie could tell by the firm set to Brad's mouth and the twitch of Alexis's right eye that neither one was happy.

"I'm going to give Image one more week here at the track with Vince," Fredericka continued. "If she doesn't show any progress by then, Brad, I'll listen to your offer."

"One week!" Melanie blurted out. This time she was the one who was stunned. One week would never be enough time to regain Image's trust and make any headway in her training. "But that's not—" Fredericka shot her a warning look, and Melanie let her words die. Out of the corner of her eye, she saw Alexis grin triumphantly.

Brad nodded. "That sounds realistic," he conceded, sounding almost happy again. "Now, my new champion, Celtic Mist, is waiting." He said the name emphatically, as if to make sure that Melanie, Alexis, and Fredericka knew which horse he was talking about. "The reporters have been watching his works with great interest. Would you like to accompany me, Fredericka?"

"You go on, Brad. I need to talk to Vince about Gratis."

"*I'd* love to see him, Mr. Townsend," Alexis said.

Mr. Townsend, Melanie thought, disgusted at the sugary way Alexis said the rich man's name. The farm manager was definitely up to something. When Melanie and Kevin had worked with Image at Tall Oaks, Alexis had kept an eagle eye on them, and she'd always given Melanie the creeps. She was sure all Alexis really cared about was Alexis. But Fredericka thought she was an excellent manager, and until Alexis did something to prove Melanie right, Melanie would just have to put up with her.

When Brad left, Fredericka turned to Melanie. "I'm sorry you had to witness all that, dear."

"I'm glad I did. But only one week, Fredericka?" Melanie frowned in worry. "What can we do in only one week?"

Fredericka sighed. "I'm not expecting too much, Melanie. But as you know, by this time of the year most two-year-olds have been in a race. I'd at least like to see Image trotting on the track."

"But Fredericka, she doesn't even trust *me* anymore, and I know her better than anyone else. She panicked when she saw the saddle. There's no way I'll have her ready for the track in one week."

"I'm sorry, but that's all the time I can give you. We both can see how miserable she is here. It wouldn't be fair to keep her here any longer. Perhaps Brad and Alexis are right, and I spoiled her so much that she'll never make it as a racehorse."

"Well, if one week's all I've got, I'll do the best I can," Melanie said firmly. "I'm not going to give up. And you shouldn't, either. Remember how well she was doing at Tall Oaks? Remember when she raced Gratis that day she got loose? He was galloping his heart out and she breezed right past him. Fredericka,

40

she could be a winner. I just know it."

Smiling wistfully, Fredericka patted her arm. "I'm glad you're optimistic. Perhaps if things were different, she would have been a champion. However, right now all I can afford to give you and Image is one week. We'll just have to hope for a miracle."

Turning slowly, Fredericka made her way across the drive to the barn office.

One week? It would *take a miracle,* Melanie thought. Image needed time and endless patience. But it was clear Melanie wouldn't have that luxury now. She'd just have to do the best she could, no matter how impossible it seemed.

Dropping the lead, Melanie picked up the saddle. It was dangerous to let the lead dangle, but she didn't want to unhook it from the halter, either. Even confined, Image was hard to catch.

Holding the saddle, Melanie stood in the middle of the stall and waited while Image eyed her uneasily. For what seemed like forever, the two stood there, watching each other.

Melanie's arms began to ache, and a fly landed on her nose. While she waited, she thought about the ten stalls she had to clean and the blankets that needed to go in the dryer. She thought about Brad Townsend's harsh words—"That filly is too spoiled ever to be a racehorse." Then she thought back to the last time she'd worked with Image at Tall Oaks. Saddling her had been a breeze. In fact, the filly had been curious and excited about everything they'd done together.

How can I get her to act that way again? Melanie wondered.

Finally Image's ears swiveled forward, and Melanie took a step toward her. When the filly threw up her head in alarm, Melanie stopped again and waited.

Her foot went to sleep, and flies buzzed around her face. She heard Julio holler, "Why aren't these stalls picked out?" Still she didn't move.

Lowering her head, Image picked at a blade of leftover hay.

"Taste good?" Melanie asked, taking one more step. Image shied sideways and stepped on the dangling lead. It tightened, pulling on her halter, and she panicked.

Nostrils flared, she lunged to the other side of the stall, her haunches knocking into Melanie. Melanie slammed into the wall, then immediately flattened herself against the boards as the filly swung around again, snorting in alarm.

For several minutes Image spun frantically in circles. Then, abruptly, she quit. Raising her head, she whinnied loudly. When an answering whinny came from outside, she rushed to the open top door and peered outside, her whole body quivering.

Melanie shook her head, her lower lip trembling. Who was she kidding? She'd never get the saddle on Image.

Clutching the saddle against her chest, she slid down the stall wall until she was sitting in the straw, her knees drawn up, her heart aching. She had to face it—Image had no idea who she was anymore. And even worse, Melanie didn't know if Image would trust her—or anyone—ever again.

The thought broke Melanie's heart.

Dropping her forehead on the saddle, Melanie let the tears flow. It was too late for her to do anything more with Image. Brad was right—the filly would be better off as a broodmare at his farm. At least she wouldn't be locked up, like a prisoner in jail, at a track she would never run on.

Just then a warm puff of air tickled the top of Melanie's head. Soft lips plucked at her hair.

Startled, she glanced up. Image was standing over her. Head lowered, she snuffled Melanie's cheeks and forehead, her nostrils blowing in and out with each breath. Slowly she worked her way down Melanie's arms and legs, sniffing curiously.

Melanie held her breath.

When Image had inspected every inch of Melanie, the filly raised her head and quietly moved away. Melanie stared at her, blinking in wonder.

Was she imagining things, or had Image's expression changed?

No, she wasn't imaging it. The glint of fear had disappeared from the filly's eyes. The pinned ears were pricked forward.

She knows who I am! Melanie thought in excited amazement.

This time when Melanie stood up, Image didn't shy away from her. She came right over, laid her muzzle against Melanie's cheek, and inhaled slowly.

"You know who I am," Melanie whispered, her voice breaking on the words. Setting the saddle down, she wrapped her arms around Image's neck, buried her face in the filly's mane, and began to sob with happiness . . . and hope.

4

TWENTY MINUTES LATER MELANIE LED IMAGE FROM THE
stall. The filly stopped in the aisle under the eaves, her
head high, and looked around with interest. Melanie
checked the girth to make sure the saddle wouldn't
slip, then patted Image's neck. Once Image had realized who Melanie was, saddling her had been easy.
Even now, the filly's gaze was soft and trusting.

Melanie couldn't stop smiling. "Let's take a walk
and find some grass," she said, clucking.

Morning works were finished, and horses were
being washed, groomed, and walked. When Melanie
and Image strode by, several people paused to stare.
Melanie was trying to remember where the grassy
spots were when she spotted Vince standing in the
office doorway, a racing program in his hand. He wore

his trademark fedora and a gruff expression. "Where are you taking the filly?" he asked, his bushy brows bunched in a frown.

"Uh . . ." Melanie felt momentary panic. She was supposed to be cleaning stalls and drying laundry. She'd forgotten that she wasn't at Tall Oaks anymore. She should have asked permission to take Image out of the stall.

"I-I'm letting her get used to the saddle," she stammered. Nodding toward the direction of the track, she added, "And I thought I'd walk her and let her graze. She's been in the stall so long, her legs have stocked up. I'm sorry, I know I should have asked if it was okay."

Vince's eyes narrowed, but then he glanced back at the racing program in his hands and waved her off. "You've got permission. Just make sure you do the rest of your job, too."

"Yes, sir." Gulping, Melanie hurried off. Vince had been his usual brusque self, but he had not told her to put Image away. She hoped that was a good sign.

As they walked past the rows of barns, Image tossed her head and pranced, delighted to be out of the stall. But she stayed next to Melanie's side and didn't tug on the lead, so Melanie remained hopeful.

"You'd better not run off," she added sternly, "or this will be your first and last walk with me."

The track was empty except for an outrider. Melanie led Image to a patch of grass on the outside of the railing. While the filly grazed eagerly, Melanie took in the sights. Keeneland racetrack was beautiful in the fall, she thought. It was lush with towering pine trees, dogwoods, and maples, their leaves turning red and gold. Flower beds, bordered by rows of hedges, had been planted with purple chrysanthemums and yellow pansies.

Melanie inhaled deeply, her gaze drifting back to Image, who was greedily cropping grass. She couldn't remember when she'd felt this happy. Not that Image would suddenly be the perfect horse. But if the filly remembered and trusted her, things just might work out.

Moving next to Image, Melanie draped her arm over the horse's withers and listened to her contented munching. If Image stayed calm, Melanie could gradually introduce her to all the new things at Keeneland. Then there was working with long lines, and backing her, and introducing her to the track. . . . Okay, so they had a long way to go, but reestablishing trust was a start.

But one week?

A feeling of gloom once again washed over Melanie. One week was so little time, and she refused to push the filly. She could only hope that once Image had a taste of being on the track with other horses, she would prove to have the heart of a Thoroughbred who loved to run.

"Melanie?"

Melanie turned. Her aunt Ashleigh was walking down the gravel path toward them, a puzzled expression on her face.

"Hey, Aunt Ash. What's up?"

"Is that Image?" Her aunt was dressed in jeans, paddock boots, and a zip-up sweatshirt. Her chin-length brown hair was tucked casually behind her ears. Melanie knew that Whitebrook had several horses running that weekend, so she guessed Ashleigh had been checking on their morning works.

"Yup." Grinning, Melanie patted the filly's chest. "Hard to believe, huh?" At dinner the night before, Melanie had explained to Mike and Ashleigh why she was working for Vince.

Stopping in front of the filly, Ashleigh crossed her arms and studied Image. "Yes, it is, considering that the last time I saw her, she was trampling some poor hotwalker."

"She was trampling me earlier today. Let's hope she's over that. Though I bet she'd make even more progress if she was at Whitebrook. That's what I told Fredericka, anyway." She looked sideways at her aunt, wondering what her reaction would be.

48

"You're probably right," Ashleigh said, but Melanie could tell her attention wasn't on Image. "Melanie, we need you to ride Raven for us this weekend. I wasn't sure what your agreement was with Vince, but I was hoping he'd still let you jockey."

"Raven? Are you sure you want me? I rode her in her last race, and we didn't do so hot."

"It wasn't your fault Raven clipped her heel coming out of the gate and then ran out of gas," Ashleigh said. "We've got her entered in another mile maiden race. If she has a clean start, she should do better."

"Okay, I'll ride her. I'm sure if you ask Vince, he'll say yes. It's just one race."

"It's not 'just one race,'" Ashleigh said. "Raven's the only horse Whitebrook has running this weekend." Walking over to the railing, she leaned against it tiredly. Then Melanie noticed the dark shadows under her aunt's eyes and realized she *was* tired.

"Are you all right?"

"Yes. It's just that things have been off schedule ever since Star got sick." A shadow of worry crossed Ashleigh's face, but she seemed to shake it off. "Raven's running in the second race on Saturday. When I see Vince, I'll make sure he understands we need you to ride her."

Suddenly it dawned on Melanie what Ashleigh was concerned about. Running a Thoroughbred farm was hard work even when things were going great, but lately things hadn't been going so well. Whitebrook hadn't had a winner in the past few weeks, and although Ashleigh had never shown it, Melanie bet that Star's illness had been as tough on her as it had been on Christina.

"Are you worried about Star?" Melanie asked.

"Always. Although he's getting stronger every day, there's no guarantee he'll ever race again. Plus it's been tearing Chris apart." Sighing, Ashleigh stared across the racetrack.

"I bet it reminds you of when Wonder was sick," Melanie said softly.

Her aunt nodded but didn't say anything. It had been two years since Wonder died, but Melanie knew that Ashleigh thought about the mare every day.

"Well, I've got to work to do," Ashleigh said.

"Me too. Julio's probably wondering where I am. I've got blankets in the wash and stalls to clean." Melanie laughed. "And I thought grooming was going to be easy."

"Nothing about horses is easy. Thank goodness we love them." Ashleigh smiled for the first time since they'd started talking. "Chin up, Melanie. I'll go ask Vince about the race right now."

When Ashleigh left, Melanie's shoulders sagged. Her aunt *was* worried, only Melanie had been so preoccupied with Image, she hadn't noticed.

On Saturday she'd try to make it up to Ashleigh and Mike by riding Raven. She needed to win for Ashleigh and for Whitebrook.

"Besides, I'd better prove to everybody I'm still a good jockey," she told Image as they started back to the barn. "So that one day Vince will let me ride you!"

Saturday morning Melanie stepped on the weight scale, her racing saddle in her arms.

"One hundred and eighteen pounds," the clerk of the scales announced.

"That's not right," Melanie said. "I always weigh one hundred and twelve."

"Guess you ain't working out enough."

"Yesterday I mucked out stalls, hotwalked five horses, bathed five more, cleaned tack, fed the horses, washed out buckets, and picked out the stalls again. This morning before I came to the jockey room, I did more of the same. You don't call that a workout?" Melanie knew she shouldn't be arguing with the clerk of scales, but she couldn't help it. Lately she hadn't been riding, so she hadn't been watching her weight. It was her fault, and she knew it.

For the first time she'd have to get in the sauna and sweat the pounds off.

"What're you so riled up about?" the clerk asked. "You're still plenty light."

Exhaling with frustration, Melanie stepped off the scales. She *was* lighter than most of the male jockeys, but since she was a bug, she was allowed to ride at a lighter weight. Plus Raven was only two years old, a filly, and small-boned, so she needed to run with as little weight as possible. Melanie's extra pounds might be the difference between a win and a loss.

And Melanie had to win.

Rats, Melanie grumbled to herself when she went into the women's locker area in the jockey room. She'd been hoping to spend a little time with Image before the race. Instead she'd be sweating it out in the sauna.

Stripping to her underpants and T-shirt, Melanie opened the door to the sauna. When she stepped inside the dark cave, the heat blasted her in the face, and she was soon dripping with sweat. Sitting down, she leaned her head against the back wall and closed her eyes.

This is *relaxing*, she admitted. After two days of jumping to attention every time Julio snapped out an order, it was nice to sit and do nothing. Besides, her muscles ached from hauling buckets and pitching manure, and the heat was soothing. She'd had no idea that grooming would be so grueling.

On Friday she had been able to squeeze in time with Image. She'd groomed her until she shone, then saddled her and took her for another walk. This time they'd walked all the way around the track, stopping to graze at different spots. Again the filly had been happy to get out of the stall and curious about every thing. When they'd come back, Melanie had bridled the filly, then paraded her in front of the office, hoping Vince would see how well Image was doing.

Because Image was being perfect, Melanie thought, her lip curling up in a sleepy smile. *Just perfect.*

"Melanie?"

Someone shook Melanie's shoulder.

"Hmmm?" Melanie tried to force her eyes open, but her eyelids were so-o-o heavy.

"Melanie, wake up. How long have you been in the sauna?"

"Here. Let's try this," a different voice said. Cold water splashed Melanie in the face. Sputtering, she sat up. Her head swam dizzily and she fell back again. When she looked up, two faces were staring down at her in concern. "Vicky? Karen? Hi," Melanie croaked. "What are you doing here, and why is my mouth so dry?"

"Because you've been baking in this heat for I don't know how long. It was lucky I came in and found you." Vicky Frontiere, a jockey, put her hand under Melanie's arm and lifted while Karen Groves, another apprentice jockey, supported her other side.

When she stood up, Melanie's legs wobbled, and she swayed against Vicky. "Whoa. What's wrong with me?"

"You're dehydrated. Come on, let's get you out of here and into a warm shower." Vicky and Karen steered Melanie from the sauna. The air in the locker room felt like ice, and Melanie shivered as she crossed the tile floor to the shower.

Still dressed in her T-shirt, Melanie stood under the beating spray of water. Letting a stream flow into her mouth, she swallowed greedily. "What time is it?" she called.

"Almost noon." Vicky called back.

Melanie grimaced. She'd been in the sauna for an hour. How stupid could she be?

"You were lucky," Karen said. "The temperature was on low. What were you doing in there?"

"Trying to lose weight. I must have fallen asleep." Glancing down, Melanie patted her stomach, wondering if she'd sweated off a few pounds. She peeked out between the curtain and the stall. Vicky was getting dressed in her silks, which meant she was probably riding in the first race. Melanie knew she'd better hurry, too.

"You should have told someone you were going in there," Karen said, flinging a towel over the rod. "Here. I took that from your locker."

Melanie turned off the water. Grabbing the towel, she dried herself off. "I know it was dumb. I was just so tired."

"I heard you're grooming for Vince," Karen said.

"*Slaving* is the correct term," Melanie said. "Actually, I don't see him much. Julio's my boss."

"Julio? He's an ex-jockey," Vicky said. "Got too big. He's still mad about it—probably takes it out on you."

"Actually, he's pretty nice," Melanie said. Then she added with a laugh, "That is, when he isn't bossing me around." She stepped out of the shower, still shivering.

"You'd better get into some dry clothes," Karen said.

Melanie nodded, her teeth chattering. Her stomach was flatter, she decided—not surprising, since she was starving. As soon as she was dressed and dry, she'd check her weight, then get something to eat.

Vicky handed her a bottle of Gatorade. "Here. This'll help."

Melanie sank down on the wooden bench. "Thanks. You guys are being so nice. Neither one of you must be racing against me."

Karen and Vicky laughed. "We just miss having feisty old Mel around," Karen said. "Nobody's been

55

giving George and Sammy a hard time."

Melanie rolled her eyes. George Valdez and Sammy Fingers were two veteran jockeys who liked to play rough. When it came to winning, they had a bunch of dirty tricks up their sleeve. "I'd almost forgotten about the track bullies."

"Well, I'd better go weigh in," Vicky said, picking up her saddle.

"Who are you riding?" Melanie asked, taking a gulp of Gatorade.

"Paycheck in the first race, Big Shot—one of Vince's horses—in the tenth, and Celtic Mist in the Blue Blood Stakes."

Melanie lowered the bottle. "You're riding Brad's horse?"

She nodded, a pleased look in her eyes. "I know you and the Townsends aren't buddies," she told Melanie. "But that is some terrific colt he's got. Of course, I wasn't Brad's first pick for a jockey. He had some big-shot rider flying in from California, but the flight was delayed because of fog, so I got a chance."

"That's great, really. And good luck—for your sake, of course, not Brad's," Melanie said.

When Vicky and Karen left, she pulled out her nylon pants and long-sleeved blue-and-white racing shirt. After she changed, she put on her protective vest and went in to the clerk of scales to get weighed again.

"One hundred and sixteen," he announced.

"Only two pounds," Melanie grumbled as she stepped off the scale. That meant a Power Bar for lunch instead of a sandwich.

She bought one at the canteen and munched on it as she watched the post parade for the first race. Right away she spotted Vicky, who wore red-and-yellow silks. Her mount, Paycheck, was number nine. As they paraded in front of the grandstand, Paycheck jigged nervously beside the pony horse. Melanie wished she could concentrate on the race, since Vicky was a terrific rider, but she was too distracted by her own thoughts.

Her mind went back to her last race on Raven. Raven was quick but not a stayer, and the stumble after they broke from the gate had affected the outcome. Melanie knew she'd have to ride a careful race to win. A mile race was over so fast that the jockey didn't have time to make any mistakes.

Picking up a racing program, she checked out the competition in the second race. When she read the entries, her heart fell. Fred Anderson was riding Peaches 'n' Cream, a filly trained by Jimmy J. Since Fred had been riding for Jimmy, his bad luck had changed and he'd had several wins. But even worse was the number five horse, Theatrical, owned by G. Neubauer, trained by Vince Jones.

Melanie groaned. When Ashleigh had asked Vince's permission for Melanie to ride in the second race, he must have known she'd be riding against him.

The call for the second race broke into Melanie's thoughts. Hurriedly she stood up, catching herself on the back of her chair when her head started to swim. She closed her eyes until the dizziness quit. Then she picked up her saddle and left the jockey room with the other riders. Catching sight of Fred, she fell into step beside him.

"How's Peaches running?" she asked. Fred was about Melanie's age and also a bug. He wore yellow-and-blue silks.

"Just peachy," Fred joked, glancing over at her. He frowned. "Are you all right? You're as white as your shirtsleeves."

"I'm more than all right. I'm ready to leave you in the dust," Melanie teased. "Just because I haven't jockeyed for a while doesn't mean I'm going to let you win. Congratulations on your last couple of races, though."

Fred beamed. "I finally earned enough money to move out of my car and into an apartment. Jimmy J's been great."

"I'm glad it's worked out." When they reached the saddling paddock, Melanie said goodbye. Ashleigh was walking Raven around the paddock. Mike was meeting with the contractor who was building Whitebrook's new stallion barn, so he hadn't been able to get away for the race.

"How's she feel?" Melanie asked when she came up beside Raven. The coal black filly had a gleam in her eye as she swiveled her head back and forth to stare at the watching crowds.

"She's keyed up," Ashleigh said. "Don't let her burn out before she gets to the starting gate. And don't let her get too far behind. It's a short race, and she's not a come-from-behind horse."

Melanie nodded. Usually Ashleigh didn't give her many instructions, so she knew her aunt was nervous about the race.

"I'll do my best, Ashleigh," Melanie said. Clamping a hand on her stomach, she ignored its growling. "Um, but I need to tell you that I'm four pounds heavier than the last time I rode her. I'm sorry. The weight crept up on me. I wasn't paying attention."

Ashleigh nodded as if she understood, but she kept her eyes straight ahead as she walked Raven into the saddling stall.

Stopping outside the stall, Melanie bit her lip. She'd been so worried about Image these past weeks that she had barely thought about jockeying. And in such a highly competitive sport, she couldn't afford to slack off. What if she blew this race?

Stepping into the stall, she handed Ashleigh her

saddle. Ashleigh set the saddle on the blue-and-white blanket, a number 4 on the side. Her aunt had a no-nonsense expression on her face, her energy directed toward making sure Raven was ready to go.

That's what I need to be doing, too, Melanie thought as she put on her helmet. *Focus on winning the race.*

She took a deep breath, almost choking when she spotted Vince Jones standing across the stable yard. He was staring intently at her, his fingers stroking his chin, deep in thought.

The blood rushed to Melanie's cheeks. She'd forgotten all about Vince. Melanie desperately wanted to be the first person to ride Image and the one to start her on the track. But it was up to Vince to make that decision. That meant he'd be watching this race—watching *her.*

If Melanie blew this race, Vince Jones would never let her ride Image.

5

MELANIE SUDDENLY FELT LIGHT-HEADED. HER LEGS STARTED to buckle, and she swayed against the stall partition. Why hadn't she eaten more before the race? Why had she gone in that stupid sauna? Two pounds hardly made a difference, and now she was so shaky she'd probably fall off Raven right at Vince Jones's feet.

"Melanie? Do you want a leg up?" Ashleigh asked.

Melanie snapped her head around. "What?"

"A leg up." Ashleigh was looking at her, a concerned expression on her face. She had already led Raven from the saddling stall. Blinking, Melanie glanced around with a dazed expression. The other jockeys had mounted and were starting from the paddock.

"Oh, right," Melanie blurted out as she buckled her

helmet strap. Hustling to Raven's side, she grabbed hold of the pommel and cantle.

Ashleigh put her hand on Melanie's shoulder. "Are you all right?"

"I'm fine," Melanie said. She didn't dare tell Ashleigh she wasn't fine, because she *had* to be fine—it was too late to switch jockeys and too late to pull Raven.

Cupping her hands under Melanie's bent knee, Ashleigh boosted her into the saddle. Raven pranced sideways, and Melanie gathered the reins. "Easy, girl."

Still holding on to the lead line, Ashleigh looked up at Melanie. "I'm all right, Aunt Ashleigh, really," Melanie assured her. "In fact, if I were you, I'd tell your friends to put money on Raven to win."

Ashleigh smiled for the first time. "I just might. See you in the winner's circle." She unsnapped the lead and stepped back. As Melanie steered Raven toward the paddock gate, she looked over her shoulder, glimpsing Vince Jones, who was walking beside Theatrical. Melanie didn't recognize the jockey, a dark-skinned guy who wore red-and-white silks. Since jockeys often moved from track to track, it wasn't unusual to see a new face.

Vince looked up, catching Melanie's eye, and she whipped her head around. "Just you wait, Mr. Jones," Melanie muttered to herself. "I'm going to show you how it's done."

When they left the paddock, Raven pinned her ears at the girl on the pony horse, so Melanie decided to ride her alone onto the track and to the starting gate. "Look at this great field of fillies," the announcer said over the speaker system. Melanie checked her goggles, perched on the front of her helmet. It was a warm day, and her protective vest was hot. Her fingers were trembling, and her skin felt clammy.

Shaking her head, she forced herself to focus. *You can do this,* she told herself, her teeth gritted. *You need to do this for Ashleigh, for Whitebrook, for Image!*

Squeezing her heels into Raven's sides, she urged the filly into a trot. Raven leaped forward, throwing Melanie off balance, then settled into a bouncy jig. In the grandstand, the crowd cheered as the announcer introduced the horses. Raven's odds were twelve to one. A grin stole across Melanie's face, and the adrenaline coursed through her. With odds like that, Raven would pay off big if she won. She hoped Ashleigh had placed that bet.

When they reached the starting gate, Melanie slowed Raven to a walk. The filly bobbed her head nervously. Before the last race, Raven had balked when it was time to load. This time, while the starters loaded the first three horses, Melanie kept talking to the filly in a soothing voice. Soon it was their turn. The starter led Raven to the narrow stall, and Melanie breathed a sigh of relief when she walked right in.

"This is it," Melanie whispered to Raven. The filly's ears flicked as she listened. Melanie rolled her shoulders back, checked her foot position in each stirrup, and drew down her goggles. Then she fixed her gaze right between Raven's ears and down the empty track.

A wave of dizziness swept over her. Quickly she clutched Raven's mane to keep from tipping sideways. The filly's front hooves danced in place, and the starter, sitting on the left side of the stall, patted Raven's cheek to quiet her.

Pull yourself together! Melanie inhaled deeply and exhaled slowly. Her head cleared; her hands grew steady on the reins.

"One back!" the starter called, letting the riders know that only one more horse needed to be loaded. Melanie leaned forward, poised over Raven's withers, her grip firm on the reins, her heart thumping wildly.

Brin-n-ng! The bell rang, the starter's gun went off, the front gates flew open, and Raven burst onto the track in a black blur of motion. Melanie crouched low, her body intuitively ready to sense the slightest bobble. But it was a clean, fast start, so she began pumping with her hands, driving the filly right to the front.

Tilting her head, she checked to her left. No one was there. She jiggled the left rein, and Raven moved toward the rail. Exhilaration filled Melanie. She was right where she wanted to be. Still, the hard part was before her—she had to keep Raven on the rail position and keep her from burning out too fast.

The field of horses thundered around the first bend. Close behind her Melanie heard pounding hooves and urgent voices. Raven ran easily, her head bobbing slightly with each stride. Melanie glimpsed Peaches 'n' Cream inching up on the right side. Fred's head was tucked as he used every ounce of strength to push his mount ahead.

The blood pounded in Melanie's ears, and sweat broke out on her forehead.

Breathe, she told herself. *Fight.*

Peaches galloped closer. Neck and neck the two fillies raced around the final bend. Melanie flattened against Raven's mane, making herself as small as possible.

"You can do it, Raven," she called, urging the black horse on with her voice. "This is your race. Don't let any of those other horses take it from you."

Beside her, Fred raised his whip hand. *Whap, whap*—she could hear the whip smack against his horse's side. Then Peaches darted forward, passing Raven, and Theatrical moved up to challenge on the outside.

Melanie bit her lip, waiting. *Don't burn her out too soon.* She could feel Raven's muscles move powerfully beneath her. The filly's neck was still arched, and her breathing was even and strong.

Suddenly a wave of exhaustion swept over Melanie. Her shoulders ached; her mouth was dry. She dropped her dirty goggles to her chest. Blinking hard, she caught sight of the final pole. The last furlong. Seconds ticked off in her head.

"It's Peaches 'n' Cream in front by half a length and Raven racing gamely on the rail, with Theatrical closing. What an exciting race, folks!" the announcer cried.

Now! Melanie perched her hands higher on Raven's neck. Rocking with the rhythm of Raven's stride, she slackened the reins and pushed the filly faster. She kneaded her fists against the filly's sweat-darkened neck. "Go, girl," she called over the screaming crowd and the thudding hooves. "Give it all you've got!"

Raven responded with a burst of speed. They roared forward, caught up to Peaches 'n' Cream, and crossed the finish line a nose ahead.

Tears filled Melanie's eyes. "We did it!" she cried, half laughing even in her exhaustion. Standing in her stirrups, she slowed the filly to a canter. Raven's nostrils flared red, and foam flew from her mouth. Melanie knew the filly had given everything she had. She also knew she'd ridden the race just right. If she had pushed any earlier, the petite filly might have burned out.

Raven dropped to a ragged trot. Melanie circled in

front of the grandstand, letting the filly relax and catch her breath. When Raven slowed to a walk, the outrider drew alongside, ready to escort them to the winner's circle. "Pretty ride," he said.

"Thank you." Melanie fell on her mount's neck. Letting her arms hang, she gave Raven a hug. "And thank *you*," she whispered.

When Melanie straightened in the saddle, her head began to pound and fireworks of color popped in front of her eyes. She grasped Raven's mane so that she wouldn't fall off. Unbuckling her helmet, she pulled it off. Her hair was plastered to her head. Her cheeks burned as if they were on fire.

"You okay?" the outrider asked.

"Yeah . . . I'm jus' hot 'n' tired," Melanie said, and even she could tell her words were slurred.

When they reached the winner's circle, Ashleigh met them, a huge grin lighting up her face. "Melanie! That was amazing!"

Melanie tried to smile back, but her lips felt wooden.

Ashleigh's smile faded. She snapped the lead to Raven's bridle. "Mel? Are you—" she started to ask, but the attendant hollered for Melanie to get off for the weigh-in.

As if in slow motion, Melanie started to swing her leg around. But her limbs were so stiff they wouldn't move; it was as if weights were hanging on her arms and legs. Then her vision blurred.

So-o-o tired, Melanie thought, her shoulders sagging, her chin dropping to her chest. *I'll just sleep for a little bit.*

Her grip on Raven's mane loosened. Slowly she slipped sideways.

"Catch her!" she heard someone cry.

Then everything went black.

Melanie opened her eyes, but her lids were so heavy she let them fall closed again.

"Mel? Are you awake?"

"Mmmpf?" Trying harder this time, Melanie forced her eyes open. Ashleigh was looking down at her, a deep furrow between her brows.

Melanie blinked. "Ashleigh? What's wrong?" she tried to ask, but something was covering her nose and mouth. She struggled up on one elbow and touched her face, feeling a mound of smooth plastic.

"Lie still," a voice said, and hands pushed her back down.

Melanie's eyes widened as a strange face leaned over her. "You have a face mask on, which is delivering oxygen," a woman said. "Nod if you understand."

Melanie nodded.

The woman glanced down at a blood pressure cuff wrapped around Melanie's upper arm. "She seems to be stabilized. I think we can take the mask off," she told Ashleigh. "Get her to drink some fluids."

The woman pulled the elastic band from behind Melanie's head and lifted off the mask.

"Wow, what's going on?" Melanie asked, sitting up. "Where am I?"

"In the back of the track's rescue squad truck. Hey, lie back down." Ashleigh patted Melanie's shoulder. "You passed out when we were in the winner's circle. Luckily the attendant and I caught you before you hit the ground."

Melanie sank back against the small pillow. The collar of her shirt had been unbuttoned, and her boots were off. "Is Raven all right?" She pressed her fingers against her temples. Her head was still pounding.

"She's fine. And so are you—*now*," Ashleigh said. "Why didn't you tell me you weren't feeling well before you raced?"

"Because I was fine," Melanie replied. "Didn't Raven's win prove it?" She grinned. "Did you bet on her?"

Ashleigh rolled her eyes. "Mel, you're not taking this seriously. You passed out. The medic said you're dehydrated."

"Okay, I did do something stupid," Melanie agreed.

"But I'm not sick. You remember the time I passed out when I was on that trail ride in the mountains? This was kind of the same thing. I didn't eat lunch, and I was tired." She told Ashleigh about the adventure in the sauna. "I'd forgotten how grueling riding in a race is, and I didn't take care of myself."

"It's lucky you even got through the race," Ashleigh said. "What if you had passed out in the middle of it? You could have been trampled."

"But I didn't. I knew what I had to do. I had to ride a great race for you and Whitebrook. And to prove to Vince that I'm good enough to ride Image."

"So that's it." Ashleigh gave Melanie a knowing look. "Vince had a horse entered in the race, too."

"Theatrical. She came in third. He was watching."

"Well, you did ride a good race," Ashleigh said. "And I know Vince watched." She tried to hold back a smile, but her eyes were twinkling.

Melanie's eyebrows shot up. "He did? Did he say anything?"

"No. But Theatrical's owner did. He said, 'Next time I want that number four jockey on *my* horse.'"

"Yes!" Melanie shouted happily, and punched the air with her fist. "That's better than Vince's saying something." She tapped her lip with one finger, suddenly pensive. "Image will be ready for backing soon. If I can only convince Vince that I'm the best one to do it . . ."

"Just remember," Ashleigh said, a warning tone to her voice, "that Vince is the kind of person who hates having anyone tell him what to do. If he puts you on Image, he has to think the decision was his."

"Good advice." Melanie sat up. She felt fine. She was ready to get up and go see Image. "How long have I been here?" she asked. "Can I go now?"

The medic was sitting on a stool by the head of the cot, writing something on a clipboard. "You've been here about an hour—you had some heat exhaustion along with the dehydration. And you need fluids before you can leave," she said. She handed Melanie a paper cup. "Drink this slowly. It contains electrolytes."

Melanie sipped the drink. "Yuck. How much of this do I have to drink?"

"As much as you can."

"Then you need lunch," Ashleigh pointed out.

Melanie shook her head impatiently. "I need to get back to Vince's barn. If I don't work today, Julio will kill me. And I have to see Image. I barely got to see her this morning, I was so busy."

"Slow down." Ashleigh laughed. "You're not doing anything until I get you some lunch. If Julio has a problem with that, I'll deal with him."

This time Melanie had to laugh. "That would be fun to watch!"

An hour later Melanie had eaten, showered, and

changed and was headed out of the jockey room. It was three in the afternoon, and Keeneland was teeming with crowds waiting for the Blue Blood Stakes, the race with the highest purse of the day. Melanie hurried to the backside and made her way to Vince's barn. Image greeted her with a low nicker.

"I missed you, too," Melanie said. "How about a nice brushing? Then I'll tack you up and we'll walk around and get used to all the excitement. One day you'll be racing, and the crowds can't make you nervous."

Image bobbed her head, as if delighted with the idea. Humming happily, Melanie groomed the filly until her black coat gleamed and her tail fanned out like a silky veil. After picking out Image's hooves, she went to the tack room for a bridle and an exercise saddle.

"Good. You're back," Julio said, striding into the tack room right after her. He thrust a grooming box into her hand. "Big Shot needs to get ready for the tenth race."

"But I'm working with Image," Melanie protested.

"Vince told you to work with her?" Julio asked.

"Well, no."

"Then you follow my orders. On Saturdays every groom is needed to prep the racehorses. Doesn't matter if you just won a race or not," he added with a hint of sarcasm.

"Gee, thanks for the congratulations," Melanie muttered.

Julio ignored her. "We're short a groom, so you'll need to take Big Shot to the paddock. You'll have to work with that black filly on your own time."

"But—"

Julio gave her a sharp look, and Melanie shut her mouth.

"He needs rundowns and a gag bit," he continued. "Before you bridle him, walk him to loosen him up and settle him down. And his owner, Mrs. Carrington, always comes to the barn to give him a good-luck kiss and a carrot before he goes for his vet check. She's a little old gray-haired lady. You'll recognize her."

"I got it." Melanie exhaled loudly as she put Image's bridle back. At least she'd had a chance to groom the filly.

When she reached Big Shot's stall, the huge colt stuck his head over the stall guard and pinned his ears.

"Knock it off, you big faker," Melanie scolded. Instantly his ears pricked and he backed up. She'd cleaned the bay's stall enough times to know that his bravado was all show.

Ducking under the stall guard, Melanie clipped a lead to his halter and began to clean him. "Save that energy for your race," she told the two-year-old when he stamped a front hoof and switched his tail. She

73

remembered that several weeks earlier, in his last race, he'd fought his jockey the whole time, ending up at the back of the field. *Which must be why Vince recommended a gag bit*, Melanie thought.

Frowning, Melanie stopped brushing and studied the colt. Like many two-year-olds, Big Shot was lean, lanky, and full of himself. But his energy was mischievous, not mean and uncontrollable. Ian had always said gag bits were a last resort.

As Melanie brushed out Big Shot's tail, she tried to recall which jockey had ridden the colt when he came in last. Then she remembered—Stan "Heavy Hands" Hamrick. Stan was a winning jockey, Melanie knew. But she also knew he was the kind that got a horse over the finish line by sheer power and force. When Hamrick had finished the race, he'd complained to everyone in the jockey room that Big Shot should have been named Big *Pain*. He'd said the colt was an undisciplined slacker who needed a harsh bit so that he'd pay attention next time he ran.

He was probably the one who had told Vince to try a gag bit.

Melanie picked out Big Shot's feet, and he nibbled the back of her jeans. When she straightened, she rubbed under his mane, and he wiggled his lip with pleasure. "You are not an undisciplined slacker. You're a pussycat. You don't need a gag bit. You need someone to sweet-talk you over the finish line."

When she finished grooming Big Shot, she went into the tack room and found a racing program. Flipping through it, she read the entries for race ten and saw that Vicky was slated to ride Big Shot. Then Melanie remembered that Vicky had mentioned earlier that she was riding him. *Perfect*, Melanie thought.

Vicky was the complete opposite of Hamrick. She was a winning jockey, too, but she had light hands and a calm, quiet way of getting horses to win. Melanie bet that Big Shot and Vicky would be a terrific match. Now she just had to figure out a way to get around the gag bit.

She finished grooming Big Shot, put a cooler on him so that he wouldn't get dirty, and took him for a warm-up walk. When she passed the office, she saw Fredericka sitting in a chair talking to someone. From the sound of the other person's voice, Melanie knew the someone was Vince. Slowing, she held her breath and listened. She heard Fredericka say Image's name, then something about selling her, then Brad's name.

Melanie's mouth went dry.

"Hey, Graham, you going or coming?" one of the grooms yelled at her. Melanie turned and saw that Big Shot was blocking the aisle in front of a stall.

"Oh, sorry," Melanie mumbled, panic welling in her chest as she led Big Shot away. Questions filled her head. Were Fredericka and Vince discussing Image's future? Why would Fredericka have made a decision so soon? It hadn't even been a week yet. Was she going to sell the filly to Brad?

Melanie stopped before going too far. She needed answers to her questions. If Fredericka was going to sell Image to Brad, Melanie wanted to know. And she needed to know right away.

As she was turning Big Shot around, Fredericka came out of the office. The older woman must have noticed the distressed expression on Melanie's face, because her own face clouded.

"What's going on?" Melanie asked, keeping her voice low so that Vince and everyone else at the barn wouldn't hear. "What were you and Vince talking about?"

"This afternoon Brad made me a very generous offer for Image," Fredericka said. Coming over, she absently patted Big Shot. "More than I expected. He thinks she'll be a wonderful addition to his breeding program."

Melanie's heart sank.

Fredericka touched her shoulder. "I didn't accept, but I wanted to let Vince know that if Image continues to go downhill, I might consider it."

"But you gave us one week!" Melanie reminded her.

"I know. And I will honor that, Melanie. I promise."
She smiled sadly. "I love Image, too. But Vince isn't very optimistic about her chances of making any progress in one week."

"How can he say that? Since I've been working with her, she's gotten so much better."

"It's still a long way from running in a race." Fredericka shook her head. "I'm trying hard to make Tall Oaks successful. That means I need to learn to make business decisions based on common sense instead of emotion." She sighed. "I know this sounds horrible, Melanie, but Image already had a bad reputation, which doesn't reflect well on the farm, either."

And I bet Brad was more than happy to point that out to you, Melanie wanted to say. Instead she said, "I understand." And she did. Ashleigh and Mike bought and sold horses all the time. Melanie knew as well as Fredericka did that it was foolish to become so attached to Image.

She just couldn't help it.

6

"THERE'S MY SWEET BOY." A WOMAN WEARING A FLOWERED dress, pearls, and a pillbox hat with a veil came toward Melanie and Big Shot. Melanie straightened, and her eyes widened. The woman had to be Mrs. Carrington, Big Shot's owner. What Julio hadn't mentioned was that the little old lady was in a wheelchair, pushed by a guy who looked like a sumo wrestler.

"Hi." Melanie halted Big Shot, who pricked his ears eagerly. "You must be Mrs. Carrington."

"Yes." Mrs. Carrington stopped her wheelchair and leaned forward, a carrot in her hand. "Come here, handsome, so I can wish you good luck."

Big Shot danced forward. Ducking his head, he gently lipped the carrot from the woman's frail hand. Melanie eyed the guy pushing the wheelchair. He

78

wore a dark suit and tie, and his gaze kept darting around the barn area.

"How's he feeling today?" Mrs. Carrington asked. Raising one hand, she motioned to the man to push her closer. Big Shot lowered his head and sniffed at her hat, then sidled next to the wheelchair so Mrs. Carrington could scratch his chest.

"He's feeling great," Melanie said. "His legs are clean, and his workout time on Thursday was good. I think he's going to run great with Vicky Frontiere as his jockey."

Mrs. Carrington nodded. "That's what I told Vince." Tilting her chin, Mrs. Carrington studied Melanie with bright eyes. "I've watched you ride many times. You'd also be a good jockey for Big Shot. That was a wonderful ride on that black Whitebrook Farm filly. You hand-rode her perfectly."

Melanie's brows shot up. This little old lady obviously knew what was going on around the track. "Thank you." Taking a chance, Melanie mentioned the gag bit. "I think Big Shot would race a lot better with a regular snaffle bit, especially with Vicky riding."

"Hmmm." Closing her eyes behind the veil, Mrs. Carrington leaned back in the wheelchair. Her head dipped to one side, and her pillbox hat drooped. Melanie wondered if she had fallen asleep. She glanced up at the guy pushing the wheelchair, who still stood at attention, his eyes straight ahead.

Suddenly Mrs. Carrington sat upright. "You seem like a knowledgeable young lady. I'll go with your recommendation. Put a snaffle on him." She kissed Big Shot one last time on his muzzle, then directed her wheelchair forward with a flick of her wrist.

S.J. came up beside Melanie, a bucket of bran mash in each hand. "You know who that is, don't you?"

"Sure. Big Shot's owner."

"Right. Also the owner of Seattle Silver."

Melanie's jaw dropped. "The colt that won the Kentucky Derby last year?"

"That's the one," he said, and walked off. Melanie groaned. *Now what have I done? Why can't I just do as I'm told? If Big Shot loses, Vince will probably fire me.* "Come on, Big Shot, let's get you walked out."

A half hour later Melanie brought Big Shot back to the stable area to put rundowns on his legs in preparation for his race. She wanted to get him all ready in time to watch Vicky race Celtic Mist for the Townsends. She'd heard so much about that colt, she was dying to see him run.

The loudspeaker announced the results of the seventh race. Finishing the last rundown, Melanie patted Big Shot and then jogged to the saddling paddock.

She spotted Ashleigh, Cindy, and Mike, who were

admiring the horses as they paraded around the oval. "Hi," Melanie called, and joined them at the rail. "Christina didn't come with you guys?"

"Nope," Ashleigh said, her eyes not leaving the horses.

Mike looked sideways at Melanie. He was dressed in khaki work pants and a navy knit shirt with a White-brook logo on the pocket. His thick, tousled brown hair made him look as though he were still a teenager, although his hands were callused and creased from hard work. "She's at Whitebrook with Star. Something about a new massage therapy she wanted to try."

"I offered to watch him, but she wanted to stay," Cindy said. She wore a denim skirt with a black turtle-neck and chunky-heeled shoes. Melanie had seen her only in jeans or sweatpants and was surprised at how grown-up and stylish she looked.

"Here he comes," Ashleigh said, pointing to a handsome dapple gray colt entering the paddock. Brad Townsend walked on his right side while a groom walked on the left. "Leave it to Brad to arrive at the last minute so he can make an entrance."

When the official stopped the colt at the gate to check his lip tattoo—his registered Thoroughbred ID number—the gray suddenly reared, lashing out with his front hooves. The groom yanked on the lead shank and quickly got the colt under control. Brad smiled up at the feisty colt as if he was delighted with his attention-getting performance.

"He's got powerful haunches," Mike commented. "But that doesn't mean he can run. Brad's convinced he's going to sweep all the pre-Derby races and go on to win the Triple Crown."

Ashleigh sighed. "Too bad Whitebrook doesn't have a hot contender to give him a run for his money."

"What about Star?" Melanie asked. Surely her aunt and uncle hadn't completely given up on Star.

Mike and Ashleigh exchanged glances. "Dr. Stevens said it would take a miracle to get him back into racing form," Mike finally said. "You know a horse has to be in peak shape to compete in any race."

"True, but don't forget the Christina factor," Melanie said. "She'll never give up on Star, and neither should we!"

Mike grinned. "Thanks for your vote of confidence, Mel. Hey, and thanks for winning on Raven." He draped his arm over her shoulders and squeezed.

"Anytime," Melanie said happily.

"So, how are you and Vince getting along?" Cindy asked. Melanie was about to answer when Cindy said, "Oh, look. There's Tommy Turner and Daniel Faraday."

"How do you know them?"

"I raced against Tommy on the West Coast. And Daniel Faraday rode at Belmont for years."

"Do you know Vicky Frontiere?" Melanie asked. "She's riding Celtic Mist for the Townsends."

"I've heard of her."

"Brad was supposed to fly in Enrico Estevan, the jockey who rode Celtic Mist to his first win in California," Mike explained. "But the flight got delayed."

"Vicky's really pumped about this ride," Melanie said. "Even if Brad is a pompous jerk," she added in a low voice.

"Let's hope Brad gives her a chance to prove herself." Ashleigh nodded toward Brad, who was walking beside Vicky. He was shaking a finger in her face, and even from the rail, Melanie could hear his stern voice. Vicky was a great rider and didn't need Brad's lecture. But from the composed look on Vicky's face, it was clear that the veteran jockey knew how to handle an owner such as Brad.

Melanie rubbed her hands together in nervous anticipation. "I don't know why I'm so excited."

"You and everybody else." Mike gestured to the large crowd that surrounded the paddock. When Celtic Mist paraded past, several people began to clap and cheer.

Ashleigh shook her head in disbelief. "I know Brad's been hyping that horse, but the Kentucky Derby is a long way off. Anything could happen between now and then."

Melanie agreed. Anything *could* happen. Star could get better, for instance, and start beating Celtic Mist in the Derby prep races. Image could even have a chance at making it to the Derby, Melanie thought wistfully.

As she followed Ashleigh, Mike, and Cindy to the grandstand, Melanie pictured Image flying along the track, leading the field of three-year-olds. The crowd would be going wild, because a filly rarely entered the Derby, and since Image was Kentucky bred, they'd be doubly excited.

Get a grip, Melanie scolded herself as she hurried into the grandstand. *Image is more likely to wind up at Townsend Acres, having babies.*

When Melanie reached the special seating area, she saw Lavinia Townsend, Brad's wife, in their reserved box. "I declare, isn't our colt just the handsomest animal out there?" Lavinia crooned to the impeccably dressed people surrounding her.

Melanie caught up to Cindy. "Lavinia probably isn't sure what kind of animal he is," she whispered, causing Cindy to burst out laughing.

Stopping by the bar, Melanie ordered a soda. By the time she reached Whitebrook's box, Ian had joined the others.

"That Townsend colt is pretty faultless," Ian was saying as they watched Celtic Mist parade past the grandstand toward the starting gate. The gray's tail was up, and the pony rider held his head snug against his leg. Up on his back, Vicky looked calm and in control.

"Yeah, but the rest of the field doesn't look too shabby, either," Mike said.

Melanie sipped her soda as one by one the horses walked into the starting box. She felt slightly guilty for taking a break from her grooming duties. She'd have to leave as soon as the race was over and get back to Big Shot. But there was just no way she could miss this.

"They're loading number four, Celtic Mist." The announcer's voice rang through the grandstand. "Will this California-bred colt replace Wonder's Star as Townsend Acres' next Derby contender?"

"I can't believe they're making such a big deal over that horse," Ashleigh said indignantly. "He's never even raced in Kentucky before."

"Brad has a lot of clout," Mike explained. "He knows how to work every angle. There has been so much publicity about the 'colt from California' that ticket sales and betting at the track are way up. The Keeneland officials are very grateful to Brad, I'm sure. Making a big deal out of Celtic Mist is one way of thanking him."

"This is a fast track today, folks, for the Blue Blood Stakes," the announcer went on. "After the race, we're going to compare the winner's time with the winning time last month in the Laurel Stakes. As you recall, that race was won by Wonder's Star. Today Kentucky may just crown a new super colt!"

"Well, I don't care how much money the track is raking in," Melanie grumbled. "I think someone needs to punch the announcer in his fat face."

"I'm just glad Christina isn't here," Cindy said, and Melanie had to agree.

"The horses are loaded," the announcer called. Instantly a hush fell over the crowd—except for Lavinia, who clapped her hands excitedly. Then the bell rang, and Melanie's heart leaped into her throat the moment the horses flew from the gate.

"Celtic Mist is off to a great start! Far East is right behind, with Lenny Two in third place. Fortune's Way and Demonic had rough starts but are making up time. . . ."

Melanie tuned out the announcer. She kept her eyes glued to the only gray horse in the field of chestnuts and bays. Part of her wanted Vicky to win. Part of her wanted the Townsends' horse to lose.

But from the way Celtic Mist was running, there was no way the colt was going to lose.

Halfway around the track, he was on the rail, a length ahead and running strong even though Vicky had him rated. Even more amazing was that the colt continued to surge ahead. Melanie knew several of the horses entered in the Blue Blood Stakes. They all had impressive records, but Celtic Mist was pulling away from the field as if the others were walking.

In the Townsend Acres box, Lavinia was waving and cheering like a high-school cheerleader. Melanie had never seen the snobby, reserved woman so giddy. "If Lavinia doesn't watch out, she's going to mess up her hair," Melanie whispered to Cindy.

"If she doesn't shut up, I'll mess it up for her," Cindy whispered back.

The announcer's voice rang out again. "Down the homestretch, Far East's jockey uses the whip, but there's no way anyone's going to catch Celtic Mist! He's driving toward the finish line with power to spare."

Beside Melanie, Mike shook his head in amazement. "Look at the stride on that colt," he said. "He's eating up the track."

"And it's Celtic Mist by three lengths, Far East in second, Fortune's Way in third. And folks, it's not official, but we have a new track record for the mile and a half!"

"Oh, no." Melanie swallowed hard when she heard the time. "He beat Star by two seconds."

"That doesn't mean—" Ashleigh started.

"Yes! Yes!" Lavinia screeched, drowning out her words.

"Well, I've gotta go be a groom," Melanie said.

"Vicky's riding Big Shot for Vince in the tenth race."

Cindy frowned. "A groom? But I thought you were riding for Vince."

"I'll tell you about it later." Melanie hurried from the grandstand. When she reached Big Shot's stall, she checked his rundowns, pulled off his cooler, and gave him a final dusting with a soft towel.

"You'd better run well with this snaffle bit," she told him as she put on his bridle. "Or no more carrots from Mrs. Carrington."

Big Shot stamped his hoof, as if in protest. When Melanie led him from the stall, he pranced eagerly. She walked him around, calming him with pats, until the announcer called for entries for the tenth race to head to the saddling stall.

Before she went, she stopped in front of Image's stall. The filly peered out through the wire mesh door. By the time the tenth race was over, it would be evening. Melanie knew she'd have to walk, bathe, and groom Big Shot, which would take at least an hour. Then there would be stalls to pick out and legs to wrap.

Sticking one finger through the mesh, Melanie stroked Image's nose. "I promise we'll have time together tonight. No matter how late it is."

And no matter how tired I am, she added to herself as she led Big Shot to the receiving barn, her feet dragging.

After the colt's vet check, Melanie hurried him to the saddling paddock. The official handed Melanie the number 6 to clip onto his bridle. "This is Big Shot," Melanie told an inspector who held a clipboard. The man lifted the colt's lip to check his tattoo, then waved them through. Melanie led the colt around the paddock. Vicky was standing by stall five, talking to Vince. Melanie caught her breath when Vince looked her way. Any minute he would notice the snaffle.

"You've got the best jockey here," Melanie chattered to Big Shot, trying to calm her own nerves. "There's Heavy Hands Hamrick. Don't worry, he's riding someone else. And look, that chestnut colt has sickle hocks, and that one with the blaze is sucking wind already. It'll be a piece of cake."

The colt rolled his eyes, danced a few steps, and kicked out, but Melanie felt that it was more from high energy than nastiness. He would go fine with the snaffle, she was sure of it. Now if only Vince would agree . . .

After a few turns around the paddock, Melanie led Big Shot to the number five stall. "Hey, congratulations on your win!" Raising her hand, she slapped palms with Vicky, who grinned happily. "What was Celtic Mist like to ride?" she asked.

"Awesome. It was like driving a race car. And I barely had to touch the gas pedal."

"That good, huh? So much for telling Christina the colt ran like an old plow horse." Melanie smoothed the green-and-black saddle pad on Big Shot's back, then took the saddle from Vicky. "Where's Vince?" she asked, nervously peering over her shoulder.

"He's got another horse running. The one in stall nine. The groom is having some trouble with him."

"Good." Haltingly Melanie told Vicky about the snaffle bit. The jockey's eyes widened under the brim of her helmet. "You went against Vince's orders?"

"I got permission from the owner," Melanie said in her own defense.

Vicky shook her head. "Vince is going to be furious."

"Not if Big Shot wins." Melanie gave Vicky a meaningful look.

"Are you threatening me?" Vicky asked, laughing.

"Definitely." Melanie's tone was teasing, but inside she was beginning to feel worried. Vicky was right. She should have asked Vince if it was all right to switch bits. But she also knew that it was unlikely that Vince would have agreed to the switch. And she was so sure that Big Shot would run better with the snaffle. She just had to keep her fingers crossed and pray that she was right.

When Melanie led Big Shot from the saddling stall, Vince was striding toward them, scowling. Melanie pretended she didn't see him. She turned on her heel and walked the colt in the opposite direction.

"Riders up!" the paddock judge shouted. Vince came over to give Vicky her last-minute instructions. Melanie had no choice but to stop.

Vince studied the horse, frowning. "Why isn't that colt wearing a gag bit?" he demanded.

"Oh, I hate gag bits," Vicky said quickly. "I'm glad he isn't."

"*Melanie?*" Vince glared at her as if he hadn't heard Vicky.

"W-well, uh, Mrs. Carrington and I—" Melanie stammered.

"Mrs. Carrington?"

"Number five horse, let's go," the paddock judge called.

"That's us," Melanie said, forcing a grin.

Vince stuck his finger in her face. "I'm not through talking to you, Ms. Graham."

"Yes, sir." Melanie's heart plummeted.

"Don't worry, Big Shot and I will do great," Vicky said when the trainer left. "Vince will forget all about it."

Melanie sighed. "I doubt it—I mean, I don't doubt you'll race well, but I don't think Vince will forget about it."

At the gate Melanie unsnapped the lead, wished

Vicky good luck, and stepped back.

"Hey, Melanie!" Melanie heard Cindy's voice from somewhere outside the saddling paddock. She peered over the crowd, which was dispersing to watch the race. Finally she spotted Cindy's waving arm.

She waved back, then followed the other grooms and trainers from the paddock. Vince had already left.

"Did you get sick of swooning over Celtic Mist?" Melanie asked. She couldn't help it—she was truly sorry Brad's colt had won.

Cindy wrinkled her nose, as if she'd tasted something sour. "You should hear Brad. He was bragging so loudly, you'd have thought he ran the race himself."

Melanie burst out laughing.

"Your colt looks good," Cindy said. "Isn't that the same jockey riding him who rode Celtic Mist?"

Melanie nodded. "Yes. Vicky."

"Wow. She must be doing great here in Kentucky." Cindy sounded wistful.

"She is," Melanie agreed as the two girls made their way to the rail. "She used to ride in California. She moved here last year. I think she and Ashleigh got to be pretty good friends back when Ashleigh was a jockey."

"So why aren't *you* riding for Vince?" Cindy asked. "I watched you ride Raven. You did a super job."

Melanie flushed. A compliment from an experienced jockey such as Cindy meant a lot. "Grooming is the only way I could be with Image." As they walked through the crowd, Melanie told Cindy the whole story.

Cindy shook her head. "I guess I understand why you're doing this, but if you and Christina ever want to make it as professional jockeys, you're going to have to concentrate on your riding." Melanie nodded silently. She knew Cindy was right, but she wouldn't have traded her time with Image for anything.

When they reached the railing Melanie leaned over it, trying to spot Big Shot. She must have looked worried, because Cindy asked, "Are you okay?"

"Yes. Well, no," Melanie admitted. She told Cindy about the switched bit.

Cindy waved her hand. "Too many trainers think they're gods. It sounds like you made a smart decision. If Vince fires you, it's his loss. But let's watch. I bet your colt does well."

"They're off!" The announcer's voice made Melanie jump. She peered around the onlookers hanging over the rail. The field of horses thundered down the straightaway in a line of brown and black. Since Big Shot was bay, he was hard to pick out. Finally Melanie spotted Vicky's green-and-black helmet. Big Shot was on the outside of the field and so far behind that Melanie could barely see him.

They galloped past, Big Shot running lazily, as if he

had all the time in the world. Melanie grimaced. At least the colt wasn't fighting Vicky, which was little consolation if he ended up dead last.

"I'm in trouble," Melanie muttered.

"Hey, the race is a mile and a half," Cindy pointed out. "They've still got a long way to go. Anything can happen."

Turning, Melanie glanced high into the glass-fronted grandstand. She knew Mrs. Carrington had to be watching, but it was too far away to spot her.

The horses charged down the backstretch. Melanie glimpsed a flash of green and black somewhere near the middle of the tightly running pack. At least the colt hadn't dropped back even further.

When the horses flew around the stretch turn, the pack began to string out. Two leaders were battling for the rail. The other horses straggled behind them.

Melanie craned her neck, trying to find Big Shot. Then she saw him, still positioned on the outside. Oblivious to the other horses, he galloped smoothly toward the finish line, as if running his own private race. Vicky sat low and quiet.

"Come on, Big Shot," Melanie yelled. "Go!"

As the colt thundered closer, Melanie saw Vicky's weight shift slightly and her hands move higher on the colt's neck. In response, Big Shot's stride lengthened.

"Wait a minute, folks. Number five, Big Shot, owned

by Ruth Carrington of Derby fame, is making his move on the outside. He's passing the third-place horse . . . now he's neck and neck with Opera Star. Feeling the heat, Angel Adkins is using the whip on the first-place horse, Premier, but the colt isn't responding. Jockey Vicky Frontiere is coolly riding her mount to the finish line, and it's Big Shot by half a length!"

Melanie's heart flew into her throat. "Yes!" Punching her hand in the air, she hopped up and down. Big Shot had won! She'd been right about the bit all along!

"See, I told you." Cindy was grinning, too. "Vince should thank you."

"I've got to go lead him into the winner's circle," she told Cindy breathlessly. "See you later!"

Weaving her way through the crowd, Melanie hurried toward the gate. Luck was definitely with her, she thought—first Raven's win, then Big Shot.

Vince had to have noticed.

The grooms of the horses who hadn't placed were streaming onto the track to take hold of their sweat-soaked mounts. Vicky and Big Shot were trotting past the grandstand to the cheers of the crowd.

Still smiling, Melanie jogged onto the track. "Congratulations!" she called when Vicky came trotting back. Vicky pulled Big Shot to a halt, and Melanie snapped the lead onto his bridle. "You did a great job."

Vicky dismounted and walked with Melanie as she

led the colt through the gate into the winner's circle. "He ran like a charm," she said, grinning. "At first I thought Stan was right—the colt was a slacker. But then I realized he was just cool as ice and ready to turn it up a notch if I asked nicely. And when I asked, he did!" she added breathlessly. Then she hugged Melanie. "Thanks. This is a record for me—the first time I've won two races in one day."

"You were awesome," Melanie said sincerely. She unbuckled the girth, and an attendant ran over to take off the saddle.

"I'll take Big Shot," a gruff voice said.

Melanie turned just as Vince took the lead line from her hand.

"And later I'll see you in my office," he added, raising his eyebrows at Melanie. Without another word, he led the colt toward the center of the winner's circle. Vicky had taken the saddle and was standing on the scales, joking with the clerk.

Melanie's cheeks reddened with embarrassment. She should have known it wouldn't matter to Vince Jones if Big Shot won or lost. She'd defied his orders, and he had every right to fire her.

Shoulders slumping, Melanie headed from the winner's circle to the barn area. She'd blown it, and there was nothing she could do except say goodbye to Image while she had the chance.

7

WHEN SHE REACHED BARN 15, S.J. WAS STANDING OUTSIDE Image's stall, a pitchfork in his hand. His face was red and sweaty. The World Is Coming to an End was written across the front of his T-shirt.

Melanie had to agree. "Hey, S.J. Is Image all right?" She peered through the mesh screen. Image stood planted in front of the doorway, her ears flat.

S.J. rubbed his upper arm. "*She's* fine. I'm not. When I went in to clean her stall, she tried to take a chunk out of my arm." Lifting up his sleeve, he showed Melanie the teeth marks.

"That's awful," Melanie said, and she meant it. There was nothing worse than working in a cramped stall with a horse you couldn't trust. She couldn't believe Image could behave that badly.

97

S.J. thrust the pitchfork into her hand. "Here. You're the only one she likes."

Melanie took the pitchfork, and S.J. stomped off. When she looked into the stall, Image's ears were pricked, and she tossed her head as if she were pleased with herself.

"That was not funny, Image," Melanie scolded. "You're supposed to prove to Vince and Fredericka that you're getting better. What if S.J. complains? Besides, Vince is about to fire me. That means you're going to have to be nice to the other grooms, or you'll rot in your own manure."

Unlatching the stall doors, Melanie went inside. "I did something really stupid, and now Vince is mad," she explained as she stroked the filly's silky neck. "But I couldn't let them put a gag bit on Big Shot. I just couldn't. He's almost as nice as you, you big dope."

Image butted her in the chest.

"But it looks like I'm going to have to say good-bye." A sob caught in Melanie's throat, and she ruffled the filly's forelock. "No matter what happens, I'll be back to clean your stall and take you out for a walk. You must be going stir-crazy. I'd do it now, but Big Shot should be here any minute, and it's my job to take care of him, too. At least, while I still have a job." Kissing Image on the nose, Melanie left quickly, before she burst into tears.

She went into Big Shot's stall, making sure it was clean and neat. Next she filled his bucket with fresh water and set it by the stall door. When that was done, she got his cooler and grooming supplies, which she also set by the stall door. Last, she filled a bucket with warm soapy water and made sure the hose was ready. The colt would be streaked with dried sweat and dirt.

By the time Vince brought Big Shot to the barn, the colt's head was hanging close to the ground. A sweat sheet had been loosely draped over him, and he was walking slowly. The mile-and-a-half race had taken its toll on the usually rambunctious colt.

Before Vince reached Melanie, he handed the lead to Julio. "Two quarts of bran mash," Melanie heard him say. "A poultice under his standing wraps. And make sure the groom gets it right this time."

The blood rushed to Melanie's cheeks. Vince hadn't even glanced her way.

When Julio brought Big Shot over, Melanie said, "I heard him. I'll do it right."

Julio cocked one eyebrow. "You'd better," he grumbled, and then walked away.

Big Shot rubbed his face on her shoulder, and Melanie scratched under the cheek piece of his bridle. "Nice race, buddy. Though you'd think someone else might say something nice, instead of being such a jerk."

Flipping up the cooler, she undid the girth. "Now let's get you comfortable."

After Melanie untacked Big Shot, she took off his rundowns, washed under his belly and between his legs, and put the sweat sheet back on. She let him have five gulps of water, then started to walk him. He needed to be completely cool before his bath.

To help make the time go faster, Melanie walked him over to the barn where Whitebrook rented five stalls. Joe Kisner was sitting on a chair outside a stall, reading a magazine.

"I hope Ashleigh doesn't catch you loafing on the job," Melanie teased.

"I'm all done for the day," Joe said, shrugging tiredly. Dropping the open magazine on his lap, he eyed Big Shot. "Is that the colt that just won?"

Melanie nodded. "How's Raven?"

"Eating like a horse." He snapped his fingers. "Hey, she *is* a horse! By the way, congrats on your win on Raven. Ashley couldn't have been happier. She was hoping to have three horses racing this weekend, but I think Raven's win made up for it."

"Thanks." Melanie stuck her head in Raven's stall, but the petite filly was too busy munching hay to notice her. "Well, I've got to keep Big Shot moving. See ya, Joe."

Melanie led the colt past several more shed rows.

They were heading back to Barn 15 when she spotted Alexis. The farm manager was striding briskly along, her head down. After glancing over her shoulder, she ducked around the corner of a shed row. Curious, Melanie followed her.

When she reached the corner, she slowed. Low voices floated from the other side. Melanie paused, tempted to listen. She knew it was wrong to snoop, but she couldn't help wondering what Alexis was up to.

She peeked around the edge of the building. Alexis's back was to her. She was talking to an older, attractive man with steel gray hair. Melanie had seen him many times before at Turfway and Churchill Downs. The man was dressed in a neat blue sport coat and tasseled loafers. *Probably an owner,* Melanie thought.

Melanie was about to duck back when she saw the man pull a long envelope from the inside pocket of his sport coat and hand it to Alexis. Without opening the envelope, Alexis stuck it in her leather shoulder bag.

Suddenly Big Shot snorted, and Melanie jumped. The man looked up, and Alexis turned around. "I thought that was you, Alexis," Melanie said, leading Big Shot around the corner, her heart thumping. "Did you see Big Shot's race? He ran great for Vicky. Vince was really pleased," she babbled.

Alexis glared at Melanie in annoyance. Melanie

knew she was chattering like a fool, but she didn't know what else to do. She stuck out her hand to the man. "Hi, I'm Melanie Graham, Ashleigh Griffen's niece," she said, introducing herself.

"Thomas Blakely," the man said.

"The owner of Fairleigh Farm?" Fairleigh was a large breeding farm outside of Louisville.

"Yes, that's right."

"I met Mr. Blakely in California," Alexis said. "My previous employer bought several of his wonderful yearlings." She gave Melanie a smug smile.

"Really?" Melanie tried to look impressed.

"Well, thanks for everything, Alexis. Ms. Graham." Mr. Blakely bowed his head. "Say hi to Ashleigh and Mike for me. Oh, and Alexis, tell Fredericka I'll contact her soon."

When Thomas left, Alexis said, "I have to go, too. I'm meeting Fredericka in her box in the grandstand. You know she met with Vince about Image earlier today," she added, her mouth tilted up in a faint smile, as if she was hiding something.

"I know," Melanie said. "She told him that Brad made her an offer that she *didn't* accept." Glancing sideways at Alexis, she tried to gauge the farm manager's reaction.

Alexis shrugged as if she didn't care, but her lips moved down into a slight scowl. Melanie knew Alexis wanted Fredericka to sell Image to Brad, but she wasn't sure why.

"Perhaps she'll reconsider. It's a generous offer for an unproven filly. Well, see you later," Alexis said hastily before heading toward the grandstand.

Slowing Big Shot, Melanie watched Alexis go. How did Alexis know what kind of offer Brad had made? Had Fredericka confided in her?

Turning, she felt the colt's chest. He was dry and cool. "Time for your bath," she told him. "Then time for me to meet with Vince—and face the firing squad."

An hour later Big Shot was clean and dry. Melanie was crouched in the dirt, slathering a poultice on his front leg, when Julio interrupted her. "I'll finish his wraps. Vince wants to see you in the office," he said.

Melanie straightened. Her back ached, and her jeans were wet. It was almost seven-thirty, and she hadn't eaten anything since the sandwich Ashleigh bought her, which seemed as though it had been days ago.

She handed Julio the poultice and bandages. "Don't mess it up," she teased.

Melanie's feet dragged the whole way to the office. When she went in, Vince was seated behind his desk. Melanie was surprised to see Fredericka there as well. She scanned Fredericka's face, trying to read her expression. Was she there to announce that she'd accepted Brad's offer? But Fredericka looked serene, as always. She nodded pleasantly at Melanie.

"Thank you for coming," Vince said, leaning forward. He paused, stroking his chin and studying Melanie intently. "As you know, Image has been . . . difficult."

Melanie was slightly confused. She thought Vince had called her in because of Big Shot's bit. Why was he talking about Image?

Folding his hands in a steeple, Vince propped his elbows on the desk. "And this latest incident made me realize that Fredericka and I were due for a conference."

So that was it. S.J. must have been mad enough to say something to Vince. "She didn't bite him hard," Melanie said.

Vince cocked one brow. "Bite? I don't know anything about any bite. I'm talking about Image kicking down her stall door."

"*What?* But I just checked on her about half an hour ago," Melanie spluttered.

"About fifteen minutes ago she put a hind foot right through the door. She's fine, except for a little scratch. We had to move her to another stall." Vince shook his head, as if disgusted.

"It's only because she hates being—"

"Let Vince speak, Melanie," Fredericka interrupted.

"Sorry." Melanie dropped her gaze.

"None of my staff cares to work with her," Vince continued. "And who knows how long it will take before she breaks out of her new stall."

"I realize that, but—" Melanie started in again, desperate to plead her case, but Vince's stony expression made her shut her mouth.

"After much discussion, Fredericka and I have made a decision that we feel will be best for Image," Vince said, sounding grim. "Fredericka, do you want to explain?"

"Yes." Fredericka pursed her lips, then took a deep breath. This time Melanie *could* read her expression, and it told her the worst.

Fredericka was going to sell Image to Brad.

"I'm taking Image back to Tall Oaks," Fredericka said.

Tears pooled in Melanie's eyes. *Image will become a broodmare. No one will ever find out if she could have been a champion.*

"I've been mulling over what you said several days ago," Image's owner went on.

I'll probably never see her again.

"Melanie? Are you listening to what I'm saying?" Fredericka asked.

Melanie shook her head. "No, I'm sorry. I'm too upset."

Standing up, Fredericka went over and gave Melanie a hug. This time she was smiling. "I said I want you to come to Tall Oaks and work with Image."

Melanie blinked in confusion. "What?"

"Even Vince agrees that you have a special way with my princess, so I'm taking your advice. Image will come back to Tall Oaks. You'll work with her there for a week, getting her ready to work on the track. Then, when Image is ready for a practice track, I'll board her at Whitebrook. I talked to Ashleigh and Mike about it this afternoon. They think it's a great idea."

"What?" Melanie repeated. She was so stunned, she wasn't sure she was hearing right.

"Of course, there have to be some limits," Fredericka added. "I can't afford to wait forever for my princess to settle down. I'll give you one more week at my farm. If you can't show me that Image has what it takes to be a racehorse, then I'm afraid no one can, and I'll just have to be realistic and forget about sending her to Whitebrook. And I'll have to accept Brad's offer."

Melanie's eyes grew huge. Grabbing Fredericka's hands, she squeezed them excitedly. "You mean it? This isn't some sick joke?"

"I mean it."

"Wow!" Melanie exclaimed in amazement. Never in her wildest dreams had she imagined that this was how things would turn out!

Suddenly Melanie caught Vince's eye, and when she saw his disgruntled expression, she reined in her excitement. "Uh, aren't you going to yell at me about the bit switch?"

"No," Vince replied almost reluctantly. "Mrs. Carrington made it quite clear that it was *her* idea, and you were only following orders. No one questions Mrs. C. Not even me." Although the trainer never smiled, Melanie thought she saw a trace of amusement in his eyes. "Now, as far as Image goes, there's only one thing I have to say," Vince said gravely, glancing from Fredericka to Melanie.

"What?" Melanie asked, her heart skipping a beat.

Vince tried to look gruff, but his lips finally twitched in a smile. "Get that filly out of my barn before all my grooms quit!"

8

"WE'RE ALMOST THERE," MELANIE SAID EXCITEDLY. SHE WAS riding with Image in the back of Vince's horse van. Crosstied in one of the narrow stalls, Image tossed her head and struck out with one hoof. The van smelled like wet manure, and the bale of hay Melanie was sitting on prickled her skin, but Melanie didn't care.

They were going home to Tall Oaks.

"Do you think your friend Pirate will recognize you?" Melanie asked the filly. Pirate was the blind ex-racehorse Ashleigh and Mike used to work with the younger horses in training. "Joe brought him to Tall Oaks yesterday so that he'd be there when you arrived. As soon as you get settled, Pirate and I are going to pony you again. Then Kevin's going to help me back you—when he can. He's still practicing for the soccer tournament this weekend."

Melanie felt the van slow down. Jumping up, she peered out the small side window. "We're turning into the driveway!"

As the van rattled and bounced up the drive, Melanie picked up the lead and snapped it onto Image's halter. The filly tried to lunge forward, and Melanie put a soothing hand on her sweat-darkened neck. "Not yet. Wait until we stop."

It seemed like forever before the van parked, the ramp was lowered, and Billy called, "Lead her out."

Image danced down the ramp, leaping the last foot. Standing in the driveway, her black coat gleaming in the sunlight, her tail streaming behind her, the filly really did look like a princess. Raising her head, she whinnied loudly. The deep bellow of a stallion answered.

Billy chuckled. "Can't say any of us are going to miss her one bit. But good luck with her," he added as he raised the ramp.

Melanie thanked him and led Image into Fredericka's barn, which was built to match her Civil War–era mansion. The wide barn aisle was flanked on either side by huge box stalls. At the end was the new stallion wing. Melanie led Image all the way through the barn and out the back double doors. The rolling fields behind the barn had been divided into spacious paddocks. Image's paddock had a run-in shed and a huge oak tree to provide shade. Pirate was napping under the tree, his tail switching lazily at flies.

Neck arched, Image seemed to float beside Melanie as they walked to the paddock. Melanie grinned, delighted to see the change in the filly already. This was where Image belonged.

When they reached the gate, Melanie led Image into the paddock. By then Pirate had heard them. He lifted his head and flared his nostrils, taking in the filly's scent. When Melanie unsnapped the lead, Image tore across the paddock, kicking, bucking, and twisting, as if trying to get rid of three weeks of misery. Climbing the fence, Melanie settled onto the top rail and watched Image's antics. The filly squealed at Pirate, raced from corner to corner, flew around the tree, then galloped back to Melanie.

Thrusting her muzzle in Melanie's lap, she stood still long enough for a quick pat before tearing off again. This time she slid to a stop in front of Pirate, and the two touched noses in greeting.

"Welcome back!" someone called.

Melanie glanced toward the barn. Elizabeth Wagner, Fredericka's full-time groom, hurried down the hill, a big smile on her face.

"Hi!" Melanie was glad to see Elizabeth, too. She'd been a good friend when Melanie had worked with

Image during the summer. "Someone's glad to be back—as you can see." She nodded toward Image, who was trotting around the paddock in an extended trot worthy of a Grand Prix dressage horse. Pirate trotted gamely beside her. Since he'd been in the pasture many times before, he already knew the boundaries. "It looks as if Pirate's glad to see her, too."

Elizabeth climbed up beside Melanie. Her long blond hair was tucked under a baseball cap. "Yeah," she agreed. "But I do know one person who's definitely not happy that you guys are back."

"Who?"

Elizabeth slanted her eyes toward the barn. Melanie followed her gaze. Alexis was standing in the doorway, one hand on her hip.

"Alexis? How do you know?"

"She told me," Elizabeth said. "This morning she was slamming feed buckets around and criticizing everything I did. When I asked her what her problem was, she said that her problem was *you*. She said Fredericka should get rid of Image, not bring her back to Tall Oaks."

"Oh." Melanie glanced back at the barn doorway, but Alexis had left. "I got the impression that Alexis wanted Fredericka to sell Image to Brad Townsend. But I don't know why. Besides, what does that have to do with me?"

Elizabeth lowered her voice. "Because Alexis is a

control freak. She hates it when Fredericka does something *she* didn't suggest. She probably thinks you talked Fredericka into doing it."

"Well, she's wrong. The only person Fredericka talked to was Vince." Melanie watched Image a minute. The filly had stopped tearing around and was grazing hungrily. "What does Alexis have against Image, anyway?"

Elizabeth shrugged. "I don't have a clue."

"Well, I hope you'll keep an eye on her when I'm not here," Melanie said. "Fall break is over, and I have to go back to school tomorrow. Luckily, my classes don't start until ten, so I can be here to work with Image in the morning."

"Don't worry. I'll keep an eye on her," Elizabeth promised. "And Pirate, too."

"Thanks," Melanie said, suddenly tired. It had been a long four days, and her exuberance had been damped by seeing Alexis once more.

Melanie hoped that she and Alexis could get along for the week Image was at Tall Oaks. Melanie had all she could handle with Image. She didn't need Alexis to make things any harder for her.

The next four days flew by. Image settled in quickly and had no trouble remembering all the things Melanie had taught her before she was taken to the track. Melanie had had no trouble tacking her up, longe lining her, and ponying her with Pirate.

It was Thursday morning, and Fredericka was coming to watch them work. Melanie had been preparing for hours. First she had hooked Image to crossties and brushed her until her black coat glowed. Then she had wrapped all four of the filly's legs in bright green polo bandages to protect them. Afterward she had tacked her up slowly and carefully, adjusting every piece of equipment until it was just so. Finally she gathered up the longe lines and prepared to drive Image down to the round pen to begin their lesson. She couldn't wait for Fredericka to see how well Image was responding to cues.

Fredericka arrived just as they were leaving the barn. "Good morning, Melanie. Good morning, princess."

Melanie halted Image, who greedily snuffled at Fredericka's hand, knowing her owner always carried treats.

"You do spoil her, Fredericka. I make her work for her treats."

"Oh, I'm saving the best treat for when Image is finished." Fredericka patted her bulging sweater pocket. "An a-p-p-l-e," she spelled out. Image tossed her head and gave a throaty nicker. Fredericka laughed. "Next she'll be learning to read."

"I hope not," Melanie said as she led the filly to the round pen. "Then she'll be really impossible."

She shut the heavy door, then straightened out the longe lines. The first time she'd tried driving Image with longe lines, Elizabeth had helped out. This time Melanie would be working the filly alone.

Fredericka peered over the high walls of the pen. "It's hard to see," she commented.

"I know," Melanie answered. "I just want to start her off here. Then maybe we can move to the pasture. I put Pirate in the barn, so he won't distract her." Melanie had already tied the stirrups down to the girth so that they wouldn't flop. She snapped the end of one rein to Image's bit ring, then ran it through the right stirrup. When she finished, she did the same for the left rein, running it through the left stirrup. Then she quietly moved behind the filly. She held both reins in her hands as if she were driving a horse and buggy. Image stood quietly until Melanie said, "Walk," and then the horse moved forward obediently. They circled the round pen, made a tight figure eight, halted, backed, and finally stopped in front of Fredericka.

Fredericka clapped her hands, beaming enthusiastically. "She was perfect. I can't believe she's the same horse that was attacking her grooms at the track!"

Melanie flushed with pride. "She's definitely happier here. But we have a long way to go. I'm supposed to be trotting her on the track by now, remember?"

Fredericka opened the gate, and Melanie drove Image down the hill to her paddock. She'd done the same thing the day before with Elizabeth as a dress rehearsal, to make sure Image wouldn't try anything silly in front of Fredericka.

They walked around the field, changing directions, and finally trotted. Image was moving along smoothly, with Melanie jogging behind, when they rounded the corner by the adjoining paddock. Out of the corner of her eye, she saw Alexis turn out two yearlings, right next to where Melanie was working with Image.

Melanie couldn't believe it. Alexis knew how territorial Image was. Why was she putting two strange horses next to her now?

Full of energy, the two colts charged across the paddock toward Image. "Whoa," Melanie commanded, keeping her voice calm. But Image had already spotted them.

The black filly wheeled toward the fence so fast that the left rein smacked her in the flank and the right rein went slack. Melanie tried to reposition herself behind the filly so that she wouldn't lose control, but she wasn't fast enough. Kicking out in surprise, Image caught her hind leg around the right rein. At the same time the colts raced down the fence line.

Furious, Image took off after the intruders. Melanie

ran with her as far as she could, then had to let go. The longe lines flapped and slapped against Image as she galloped down the fence. When she reached the corner, she slid to a stop to touch noses with one of the colts. He squealed, and Image bellowed and struck out.

Melanie held her breath. "Whoa, pretty girl," she crooned as she walked toward Image. Her heart was banging in her chest. Image didn't seem to be at all afraid of the flying, flapping reins. She was more intent on the interlopers. But Melanie knew that if the filly took off again, the reins could get dangerously tangled around her legs.

Reaching over the fence, Image pinned her ears and bit at the colt, who backed up in surprise. Melanie pulled a carrot out of her pocket and held out her hand. She inched toward Image. Three more steps.

Suddenly the two colts whirled and raced back down the fence line. Image spun to follow them, and Melanie froze as the filly charged toward her, her nostrils flared and her ears pressed fiercely back against her head. At the last second Image skidded to a complete halt. Ears pricked, nostrils blowing, she lipped at Melanie's hand, which was clutched in a sweaty fist around the carrot.

"Oh, Image." Melanie blew out the breath she'd been holding. Opening her hand, she fed the filly the carrot and grabbed the longe lines firmly, pulling them away from the filly's legs. She gave the filly a quick once-over and was relieved to find her unhurt. She looked up to see Alexis striding across the adjoining field, an exaggerated look of concern on her face.

"Melanie! I'm *so* sorry! I had no idea you were working Image down here. I thought you were in the round pen."

Melanie eyed Alexis warily. The farm manager's explanation sounded so sincere, Melanie almost believed her.

Almost. Then she realized Fredericka was within earshot. Alexis's apology was for *her*, not Melanie.

"That's okay," Melanie said. "Image has to get used to other horses someday."

"I'm glad you're not upset," Alexis said. "Give me a minute to catch these guys. I'll turn them out in the field by the driveway."

Which is where they should have been in the first place, Melanie thought, but aloud she said, "Don't worry about it. We're all finished. I think Image has had enough for one day." She led Image back to the gate. Fredericka was frowning with concern. "Are you two all right?"

Melanie nodded. "I think so. Sorry about that," she answered shakily.

"Oh, you shouldn't be sorry at all," Fredericka said. "I was glad to see Image's little tantrum."

"You were?"

117

"Image didn't care one bit about the longe lines," Fredericka explained. "She just wanted to chase off those trespassers." The older woman smiled fondly at her horse. "You little she-devil," she crooned. "But when she saw you, Melanie, she stopped on a dime. I may not know everything about horses, but I was impressed. It could have been a dangerous situation, but Image was in perfect control. Now, if we can only channel that energy into racing"—she smiled at Melanie—"we'll have a winner."

Melanie smiled back, supremely grateful that Fredericka wasn't upset. If she was right in guessing that Alexis had turned those colts out to make Image and Melanie look bad, Alexis's plan had backfired. *Thank goodness.*

"Ian's going to be here tomorrow," Melanie told Fredericka. "He's going to watch me work with Image and tell me if she's ready to be backed. I think she's ready," she added breathlessly. "I really do!"

Reaching up, Fredericka ran her hand down the snippet of white on Image's nose and nodded slowly before turning to Melanie with a smile. "I do, too. And I'm so glad you're going to be the one to do it."

After working with Image, Melanie hurried home from Tall Oaks and jumped in the shower. That night she was going with Kevin, Lindsey, Christina, and Christina's boyfriend, Parker Townsend, to see Henry Clay High School's production of *Grease*. Their friend Katie Garrity had one of the leads.

While she blow-dried her hair with one hand, she rummaged through her closet with the other, trying to find something trendy and feminine to wear. She was sick of jeans and sweatshirts.

"Chris? What are you wearing?" she called down the hall. When there was no answer, Melanie turned off the blow-dryer and padded barefoot into her cousin's room. Chris had obviously rushed to get ready, too. Dirty clothes were heaped on the floor, and clean clothes were strewn across the bed.

Melanie listened but didn't hear any voices in the house. Then she peered out Christina's window, which overlooked the barns. She could just make out Dr. Stevens's vet truck in front of the barn where Star was quarantined.

Melanie's pulse quickened. She hoped Star was all right.

Hurrying, Melanie pulled on a black denim miniskirt and red sweater. She brushed on blusher and mascara and dabbed on lipstick. Then she checked the results in the bathroom mirror. She hadn't worn makeup in so long that she'd almost forgotten she could look half decent.

After running a comb through her hair, she snatched up a pair of black clogs and ran downstairs. By the time she reached the barn, Dr. Stevens was walking out, his medical bag in his hand. Ashleigh was right beside him. They were discussing something in low, serious tones. Melanie hurried into the barn, tripping over the tanbark in her clogs.

"Chris?" Her cousin was in Star's stall. She was dressed for the play in a tan skirt and rust-colored jersey top. Her auburn hair curled on her shoulders in soft waves. "Is Star all right?"

Christina nodded. "We just had a scare. His temperature went way up. Dr. Stevens said he may still have a trace of infection in his system, so he's started him on another course of shots." Christina choked back a sob. "And I thought he was getting better. It seems like whenever I get my hopes up, something else happens," she added. She wiped her eyes with the back of her hand, smudging her mascara.

Melanie swallowed a lump in her throat as her heart went out to her cousin. It *had* been a long battle. "You know you can't give up, Chris. Star's too important."

Christina smiled shakily. "I know."

"Hey, where are my two dates?"

Melanie turned at the sound of Parker's voice. He came whistling down the aisle, but when he stopped in the doorway of the stall, his smile faltered. "Chris? Is everything all right?"

Christina nodded, but her eyes filled with tears again. Parker strode into the stall and put his arms around her. Melanie decided to leave them alone for a moment. "Uh, Chris, I'll go wait in Parker's truck."

As she headed out of the barn, she said hello to Dr. Stevens. He was giving Ashleigh a handful of disposable syringes and a bottle of medicine. Melanie knew this was Star's second course of shots. She hoped it would do the trick and that Christina would really fight to get Star back in shape once more.

Not that Christina would ever give up. In her own way, her cousin was just as stubborn as Melanie was.

A smile played over Melanie's lips as she walked back to the house. How many times had she thought about giving up on Image?

Too many to count, she decided. But something told her that Image was worth every ounce of trouble, every battle she had to fight. In fact, that was what had drawn her to the filly in the first place—they were two of a kind. And ever since she'd met Image, Melanie had dreamed about being the first person to ride her. The next day, if Ian gave the go-ahead, that dream was going to come true.

IAN WALKED AROUND IMAGE, HIS BROW FURROWED AS HE studied her. Melanie held her breath. It was Friday morning, and Ian had driven Melanie over to Tall Oaks. He'd watched her groom, tack up, and longe line the filly in her paddock. Now they were in the round pen. So far Ian hadn't said a word. He ran his hands down Image's flank, flapped the stirrup leather, whacked the saddle seat, growled, and threw up his arms.

Image twitched and flicked her ears, but she didn't shy or step aside. Melanie let out her breath. The filly was behaving better than she could have hoped for. "Well?" she asked Ian.

Ian stroked his chin as if deep in thought. "I just can't figure it out," he said, sounding puzzled. "Last

122

time I saw this horse, she was at Turfway trying to bust out of her stall. How'd you do it?"

"Oh. Well, I don't really know," Melanie admitted. Which was true. She didn't know why Image responded to her so well. It was like not knowing why a certain person was your best friend. "Maybe it's because we're so much alike. Stubborn and unpredictable." Melanie meant it as a joke, but Ian nodded thoughtfully. "What I do know is that she hates being confined to a stall," she added, waving her hand to indicate Image's paddock. "As soon as she came back here, she was a different horse. I just gave her treats. And love. And patience, I guess."

"That'll work." Ian nodded again. "Too many trainers are in it for the fast buck. That ruins horses, because they feel like they're being *forced* to run instead of running for the love of it." He glanced at Melanie. "That's what made Star a winner. He ran because he loved it."

"And he ran because he loves Christina. Which is what will help him get better."

"I hope you're right," Ian said. "So, what do you think?"

"I think Star's going to get strong enough to race again. I think he's going to run in the Derby."

Ian flapped his hand impatiently. "No, not Star, Image. Are you ready to get on her or not?"

Melanie's body tingled all over, and she gasped

with excitement. "Oh, yes. I'm ready. I just don't want to push her. Are you sure she's ready?"

"Melanie, if you're going to continue to train her, you need to trust your own judgment."

Melanie swallowed hard. "I think she's ready," she said, adding, "But only if you agree, Ian. You've had so much more experience."

Ian chuckled. "Relax. She's ready to give you a leg up herself. Come on, let's do it."

"Now?" Melanie's voice squeaked. She'd been waiting so long for this moment, she could barely believe it was finally happening.

"Now." Ian took the lead from her. Melanie checked the girth and lowered the stirrups. She couldn't believe she was getting ready to get up on Image's back!

"You know the drill," Ian said. "First just lie over the saddle. My hand will be on your leg in case she does something stupid. If she's quiet, I'm going to boost you all the way up. And don't forget to breathe. I don't want you passing out on me."

Melanie smiled nervously and nodded. Standing on Image's left side, she reached up to the saddle cantle with her right hand and the pommel with her left. Suddenly Image seemed gigantic, and a wave of doubt swept through her. She'd worked so hard to get to this point. What if something terrible happened?

"Ready?" Ian asked.

Pushing the negative thoughts out of her mind, Melanie composed herself. "Ready."

Stooping, Ian put one hand under her knee. "On the count of three. One, two, three."

Ian lifted her effortlessly into the air, and Melanie landed on her stomach over Image's back, her head hanging on the right side. Ian held her ankles and steadied the reins.

"Whoa, girl," she heard Ian say.

Tilting her head, Melanie could see Image's right eye. It was rolled backward, looking at her. She felt the filly's muscles grow rigid and her back hump. Melanie patted her shoulder. "It's me, silly. The person who feeds you carrots."

Image let out a sigh and relaxed.

"That was easy," Ian said. "Go ahead and sit up. Don't put your feet in the stirrups. If she does something stupid, just bail out. I'll catch you."

"She's not going to do anything stupid," Melanie said with certainty. Ian gave her a push, and Melanie swung her right leg over the cantle. When she sat up, her head swam as the blood rushed out of it.

"Okay?" Ian looked up at her.

"Okay," Melanie said. Then it hit her that she was finally riding Image. "*More* than okay." Reaching down, she patted the filly's neck. Image turned her head and inspected Melanie's shoe, which dangled by

125

the filly's belly. She nibbled on the toe until she got bored, then turned back around.

"Hang on," Ian said. Clucking, he led Image forward at a walk. The filly's stride was long and smooth. Melanie couldn't believe how fantastic it felt to finally be riding Image after all this time. For a second she closed her eyes and pretended she was on the racetrack, the sun and wind against her cheeks as she and Image streaked for the finish line.

Then Ian began to jog. Image broke into a trot, and Melanie snapped her eyes open, grabbing mane. "Ian, what are you doing?" she asked, her voice cracking.

He laughed. "She's like an old school horse," he called over his shoulder. "I wanted to see what she'd do with you bouncing all over her back. Whoa," he said, and Image stopped.

When Ian turned and looked up at Melanie, his smile was as broad as hers. "Perfectly quiet. Mel, you've done such a terrific job on her ground work, and it's obvious she trusts you completely. The next stages are going to go quickly. Congratulations—I don't think you have anything to worry about."

Melanie flopped down on the filly's neck and gave her a hug. "I can't wait to tell Fredericka how good she was," she told Ian. "I want to start trotting her on Fredericka's little track soon. It's not very big, but once Image gets a feel for the track, I know she'll love it!"

• • •

"Go, Cougars!" Jumping up from their seats on the bleachers, Melanie and Christina cheered Henry Clay's soccer team. It was late Friday afternoon, and Parker had driven them back to the school to watch the last of the tournament games. Henry Clay was tied with Clifton High, 4–4. It had been a close game, and Melanie had been cheering so loudly, she was hoarse.

Ian, Cindy, Lindsey, and Beth, Kevin's mom, were sitting in the row in front of Christina, Melanie, and Parker. Breathless with excitement, Melanie watched as Kevin dribbled the ball toward the goal, aimed, and kicked. The ball flew straight toward the net, but at the last second the goalie leaped into the air and punched it away. A Clifton forward retrieved the ball and sent it heading back toward the Cougars' goal. Melanie gnawed on a fingernail. There were only seconds to go. If Clifton scored a goal, they would be the champions.

Kevin tore after the ball, his legs pounding. Suddenly he stumbled, and Melanie saw him wince with pain. He dove to the ground, caught himself with his shoulder, and rolled several times before slowing. When he sat up, he was holding his knee—the same one he'd injured working with Image.

Wild cheers erupted from Clifton's bleachers.

127

Melanie jumped up. They'd made a goal. The score was 5–4. Clifton had won.

In front of her, Beth gasped. "Oh, no! Kevin's injured his knee again."

Kevin cradled his knee, his face tight with pain. The Cougars' coach was headed toward Kevin, and two of his teammates had crouched beside him.

"I hope he's okay," Melanie said, and put her hand on Beth's shoulder.

Lindsey shook her head in frustration. "I can't believe they lost. If Kevin hadn't fallen, he would have stopped the ball. We could have gone into overtime."

"It's just a game, Lindsey," Melanie reminded her.

"It's not just a game. It's the championship," Lindsey declared. Melanie liked Kevin's new girlfriend, but Lindsey played on the Henry Clay girls' soccer team and was just as competitive as Kevin.

"Besides, if one of your best racehorses lost a race because he fell, would you just shrug it off?" Lindsey countered.

"Okay, you've got a point." Melanie raised her hands in mock surrender.

Lindsey shook her head. "I'm sorry," she apologized. "I get a little wound up."

"A *little*?" Parker teased, and everyone laughed.

"I'm going down there," Lindsey said, making her way along the narrow bleacher.

"I hope his knee is all right," Beth said worriedly. "He's worked hard to get back in shape ever since that horse knocked into him."

Melanie flushed, knowing "that horse" was Image.

Ian put his arm around Beth's shoulder. "Don't worry. He'll be okay."

"But what if he's not?" Beth asked. "If he can't play college soccer, he'll lose his scholarship."

A lump stuck in Melanie's throat and her gaze shifted back to the field. Kevin's coach was helping him to his feet.

"Do you think we should take him back to the doctor?" Beth asked.

"Probably. But let's see what the coach thinks." Taking his wife's hand, Ian led her down the bleachers.

"Well." Melanie let out a big sigh. Most of the other onlookers had left as well. Cindy, Christina, and Parker were the only ones still sitting. "Just when I was feeling so good about Image. I'd forgotten all about Kevin's knee." Heaving a sigh, she plopped down beside Cindy.

"Beth wasn't blaming Image," Christina said.

Cindy agreed. "She's just worried about the scholarship. Think how bummed Kevin would be if he couldn't play sports in college." Her hand went to her own shoulder, and Melanie winced. She'd forgotten all about Cindy's shoulder, too.

"Have you decided anything?" Christina asked Cindy.

"Me?" Cindy asked. "About what?"

"Your shoulder," Christina clarified. "Aren't you thinking about an operation?"

A shadow crossed Cindy's face. "I don't know. The doctor can't guarantee I'll be able to ride again."

"And what are the chances that you'll ride again *without* the operation?" Parker asked.

"It could heal on its own," Cindy said, so forcefully that Melanie wondered if she was trying to convince herself.

"Not likely," Parker said. "The rotator cuff is—"

Cindy stood up. "I know what it is," she cut in. "You don't have to tell me. Can anyone give me a ride back to Whitebrook? I had my fill of high school twelve years ago. I don't need to hang around any longer."

"Uh, yeah, I'll give you a ride," Parker offered.

"Great. I'll meet you by the truck."

"I'll bum a ride with someone else," Melanie said, knowing they couldn't all fit in Parker's truck.

"I didn't know she was so sensitive about it," Parker said when Cindy was out of earshot.

"Think about it, Parker," Melanie said. "All these years she's been a winning jockey, traveling all over the world, totally independent. Now she's stuck at Whitebrook with her parents."

"Better than being stuck at Townsend Acres with *my* parents," Parker joked, making Melanie laugh. It was no secret that Parker and Brad and Lavinia Townsend were at odds most of the time. Melanie glanced over at Christina, who was staring off into space. She had dark circles under her eyes.

Melanie waved her hand in front of her cousin's face. "Chris? Are you all right?"

"I was just thinking about Cindy. I understand why she's having such a hard time. All she's ever known is horses. Take that crack about high school. I remember Beth saying how much Cindy hated school."

"Yeah, I can relate to that," Melanie said. "But why won't she have the operation? Especially if it might get her back on the track again."

"The risk, I guess. Like she said, there's no guarantee. At least now she can still help with morning works. With her arm in a sling, she won't be able to do anything for quite a while." Christina glanced at her hands, which were folded in her lap. "Plus it's kind of the same thing with Star. What if he never makes it back to the track?"

Melanie touched her cousin's arm. "Then he'll made a great addition to Whitebrook's new stallion barn. He's got terrific breeding and a great record."

Christina nodded sadly. "You're right. I mean, Star is valuable to me no matter what happens."

"If only Cindy could think like that, I'm sure she'd be happier," Melanie said. "This morning on the way

131

to Tall Oaks, Ian was telling me what a great job she's done with morning works. He said she really knows how to get the best out of a horse. I know he's proud of her—even if she never races again."

"Are you guys coming?" Cindy hollered from the parking lot.

"You guys go on. I'll catch a ride with Ian and Beth," Melanie said.

"Are you sure?" Christina asked.

Melanie nodded. "I want to see how Kevin is, anyway."

When the two left, Melanie dropped her chin into her hands. A breeze blew across the soccer field, ruffling her hair. The lights had come on around the parking lot, and Beth's car stood empty, so there was no hurry yet. They were probably inside talking to Kevin and the coach. Crossing her fingers, Melanie hoped that Kevin would be all right—that *everybody* would be all right, including Cindy and Star.

She thought about how alike she and Cindy were. Cindy had been a runaway foster kid until the McLeans had adopted her. Before that, she'd been in a lot of trouble.

Melanie hadn't been a foster kid, but her mom had died. After that, she and her dad had had a rocky relationship, and Melanie had been on her way to getting into a lot of trouble. Moving to Kentucky and discovering racing had been the best thing that had ever happened to her. Just like Cindy, she'd devoted herself to becoming a great jockey.

What if something happened to her and she couldn't ride anymore?

Everything about horse racing was risky. Backing a horse was just the beginning. As Image's training progressed, Melanie would take greater and greater risks. There was learning to break from a gate, galloping at high speeds on a track with other high-strung horses going equally fast, and the risk of sudden injury.

Fortunately, once Image got to Whitebrook, Melanie would have help. But she hadn't made it there yet. What about the last few days at Tall Oaks? If Melanie was going to prove to Fredericka that the filly was racing material, they had a lot to accomplish in only a few days. Elizabeth was going to be busy with the yearlings, Alexis had made it clear she wanted nothing to do with Image, and Ian had too much to do at Whitebrook—helping that morning had been a favor.

I'll just have to work alone, Melanie thought. Riding a young, inexperienced horse alone was dangerous, but she had no choice. If she couldn't trot the filly around the track by Sunday, Fredericka could still decide to sell Image. It was a risk worth taking.

10

"MELANIE!"

Melanie's thoughts were interrupted by someone calling her name. Ian was waving to her from the parking lot. Jumping up, Melanie started down the bleachers. Beth, Kevin, and Lindsey were coming out of the double doors that led to the high-school gym area. Kevin was hobbling on crutches, and a support bandage was wrapped around his knee.

Melanie let out a groan. Kevin didn't look good.

She jogged across the field, catching up to Kevin before he reached the car. She must have looked crestfallen, because Kevin said quickly, "Don't worry. The crutches are just a precaution. I was walking okay, but Coach didn't want to take any chances."

"Sorry about the game."

Kevin shrugged. "We came in second in the tournament. That's not too shabby." Stopping, he said in a low voice, "I think Mom and Lindsey are more upset than I am. But hey, it *is* just a game."

Melanie laughed, realizing it was the exact same thing she had said. "Give it up; you'd kill to win."

"Hey, I've got my scholarship. My knee just needs time to heal, which I can do this winter."

"What about basketball?" Melanie asked as she walked beside him to the car.

"I may have to sacrifice basketball if I'm going to concentrate on soccer in college," Kevin said. When they reached the car, Lindsey was holding the door open.

"What's this about basketball?" she asked.

"I was telling Melanie I probably won't play this year," Kevin explained.

"He's going to help me with Image instead," Melanie joked, though she wished it were true.

"Oh, no, he's not," Beth said. "He's not going near that horse again."

"That's right," Lindsey agreed. "He's going to be too busy cheering for the girls' basketball team—I'll be starting forward this year."

"No way," Ian said from the front seat. "He's going to study. He could lose his scholarship if he doesn't."

Kevin's head was going back and forth as if he were watching a tennis match. "Hey," he finally said. "Don't worry, I can do it all."

"Except help with that horse," Beth repeated.

Melanie knew that Beth wasn't being mean or blaming Image. She'd probably heard nothing but bad stories about Image, and when Kevin had injured his knee, she had been distraught.

Before he slid into the backseat, Kevin winked at Melanie. "Don't listen to my mom," he whispered. "I'd love to help you with Image again."

Beth and Lindsey gaped at him, and Melanie stifled a laugh. She should have known Kevin wouldn't listen to anyone else. He'd always done exactly what he wanted. Now that she knew he was willing to help, she suddenly felt a lot more optimistic about getting Image out on the track.

"She sure has come a long way since I last saw her," Kevin said. He was leaning over the pasture fence, watching Melanie drive Image in the longe lines. It was Saturday morning. Kevin had picked Melanie up right after breakfast, and they'd driven to Tall Oaks. His knee was still sore and wrapped in a bandage, and he was walking with a slight limp.

"Actually, she got worse when she was on the

track," Melanie pointed out. "But she didn't forget anything. Whoa." She halted the filly, then made her back up. "I'm glad you can help. I've got two days left. On Monday Fredericka's going to watch me trot Image around Tall Oaks' practice track. After that, she will decide if Image can go to Whitebrook."

"What makes you think she won't fall apart at Whitebrook like she did at the track?" Kevin asked.

Rolling up the longe lines, Melanie walked to Image's head and fed her a carrot. "Good girl," she said, and unsnapped the reins. "Well, at the track she was cooped up in a stall all day. Whitebrook will be just like here. She'll stay outside in her own paddock with Pirate."

"What do Mike and Ashleigh think about that?"

"They know it's unusual. But they also know that Image is different. They respect that."

Kevin chuckled. "That's saying it nicely. They just don't want her shredding their stalls."

Melanie stuck her tongue out at him and stroked the filly's glossy neck. Then she draped the coiled lines on a fence post. "Ready?" she asked Kevin.

"Ready." Kevin came in through the gate. When he took the lead from Melanie, Image gave him a thorough sniffing. Then she stuck her nose in the air and curled her top lip, making a terrible face.

Melanie laughed. "I think she remembers you."

"I don't smell that bad," Kevin huffed, and Melanie laughed even harder.

She stood on Image's left side, and Kevin gave her a leg up. "This time, if she's going quietly, I want you to unsnap the lead and let me steer her with the reins," Melanie instructed as she settled in the saddle. "I want to really ride her."

She had tacked up the filly with one of the larger exercise saddles, and her stirrups were long, so that she could wrap her legs around Image's barrel to hang on.

"Don't forget leg aids," Kevin reminded her. "She's probably very sensitive. You want her to get used to some leg so that if you accidentally bump her, she doesn't go ballistic."

"Why don't we do some of that now?" Melanie suggested. Dropping her feet from the stirrups, she let them hang against the filly's sides. When she swung them back and forth, Image jumped. Kevin held her steady, and Melanie patted her neck. "Easy, girl. It's just me."

When Image quieted, Melanie leaned forward and fed her a carrot. Then she stuck her feet back in the stirrups. With Kevin leading, they made a few circles around the pasture. Next he unhooked the lead and remained by Image's head, still walking. Like that, they went around again.

"Okay, now stop," Melanie whispered to Kevin. He

halted, and Image halted. Melanie gave her a slight squeeze with her heels. "Walk," she said, using the same command and tone of voice she used when driving. The filly scooted forward, a little surprised, then relaxed and walked around the pasture as though she'd been a trail horse all her life.

Melanie caught her breath. Image's mouth was soft and giving, her stride long and smooth. Her ears were pricked and her eyes calm. Although they were only walking, Melanie could feel the horse's powerful muscles ripple beneath her, and a thrill of excitement rushed through her. She was doing it!

She steered Image in a small circle, cut across the pasture, and then went around the shed. "Whoa." Melanie halted the filly in the middle of the pasture. Gathering the reins, she dismounted. She looked up at Kevin and laughed out loud. "Yes!" she crowed.

Kevin gave her a thumbs-up sign.

Digging in her pocket, Melanie pulled out her last carrot and fed it to Image. The filly wiggled it around with her tongue until it was behind her bit, then munched happily. Melanie couldn't stop smiling. Wrapping her arms around the filly's neck, she placed her cheek against her warm skin.

She'd ridden Image, and it had felt as wonderful as Melanie had always dreamed it would.

Now she had to ride Image on the practice track.

She had to prove to Fredericka—to everyone—that Image was ready to be a racehorse.

Melanie propped her head up. Mr. Wyman, the English teacher, was droning on and on about David Guterson, the writer. The class had been reading and discussing his book *Snow Falling on Cedars*, which had won the PEN/Faulkner Award.

Boring, Melanie thought. Every night the previous week she'd gone to bed with good intentions of reading a chapter. Every night she'd fallen asleep with the light on and the book open across her face.

Now she was having trouble paying attention, because she couldn't think about anything except Fredericka's coming to watch Image. What if the filly misbehaved? What would Fredericka decide to do?

"And now for a pop quiz." Mr. Wyman held up a sheet of paper.

Everybody in the class groaned, but Melanie groaned the loudest. Fortunately, Christina had read the book the year before and had told Melanie about it—maybe enough for Melanie to fudge an answer. If she could just get through English, she could relax. The next period she had driver ed with Christina and Katie Garrity.

That day they were taking a practice driving test,

and Melanie couldn't wait. If she and Christina did well, Mike had promised to take them to the Department of Motor Vehicles to take their *real* test. Melanie was always having to bum rides to Tall Oaks, and it was getting old. If only she could figure out a way to get her own car.

Mr. Wyman walked by and dropped the quiz on her desk. The sheet was blank except for two short questions: *Do you believe Kabuo Miyamoto is guilty? Why or why not?*

Melanie grimaced. Who was Kabuo Miyamoto? She stuck her hand in the air and waved it.

"Yes, Melanie?"

"Is this open-book?" she asked.

Mr. Wyman shook his head. "I believe we've discussed this enough in class."

"Oh." Melanie plopped her chin back on her hand. *Maybe I wasn't here those days*, she rationalized. *Or maybe I was thinking about Image.*

Sighing, Melanie picked up her pen.

Thirty minutes later the bell had rung and Melanie was searching the crowded halls for Christina. When she finally spotted her, she waved.

"Ready for your driver ed test?" Christina asked when they caught up to each other.

"Boy, am I," Melanie said. "Hey, who is Kabuo Miyamoto? You know, in that book *Snow Falling on Cedars*?"

141

When Christina told her he was one of the main characters, Melanie groaned. "When he grades my paper, Mr. Wyman is going to think I read a different book. Just what I don't need—another F to impress my father with."

"Does he still think you're going to college next year?" Christina asked.

"He keeps sending me applications from all the colleges in New York. Do you think that's a hint?"

Christina giggled. "You're going to have to tell him sometime."

"I will—*after* he buys me a car for Christmas," Melanie replied, also giggling.

When they reached driver ed, they found seats on either side of Katie. Melanie hummed a few bars of the song "Summer Nights" from *Grease*.

"Don't remind me. I really miss rehearsals," Katie said. "They're already having auditions for *Annie Get Your Gun*. Why don't you try out, Christina?"

"What about me?" Melanie protested.

Katie laughed. "I've heard you sing."

Christina shook her head. "I don't think so, Katie. I know you love acting, but it's not my thing. Besides, Star is going to need me."

"How's he doing?" Katie asked.

Christina shrugged. "This last course of antibiotics has brought his temperature down, and he's eating better."

Katie frowned in sympathy. "I hope he gets better

soon. I barely see you anymore. In fact, I hardly see either of you guys. Remember the old days when we used to go on trail rides together?"

Melanie glanced at Christina, who was smiling wistfully.

"Yeah. Sometimes when I'm keeping Star company, I talk to him about taking long rides in the woods," Christina said almost dreamily. Then a frown suddenly darkened Christina's face, and Melanie wondered what her cousin was thinking about.

"Don't you think Star is going to get better?" Melanie asked. "What does the vet think?"

"I don't know. But I'm not giving up. Today I'm going to try acupressure. It's like massage, but it concentrates on certain points on the body."

"There's acupressure for horses?" Katie asked.

Christina nodded. "It helps increase blood flow and gets rid of toxic stuff inside the horse's body."

"Would you like some help?" Melanie asked, though she hated giving up time with Image. "I don't need to be at Tall Oaks until five."

"Sure," Christina said, sounding relieved that Melanie had offered. "I've never done it before, so I'm going to need someone to hold Star and read to me from the instruction book."

After school, the girls got a snack from the house, then headed for the barn. "We need to find Uncle Mike and tell him we both passed our practice driving test with flying colors," Melanie said. "I want to make sure we can take the real test next weekend."

"What suddenly got you so excited about taking your driving test?" Christina asked.

Melanie shrugged. "I got sick of begging rides to Tall Oaks."

"You're still going to need a car," Christina reminded her.

Melanie took a huge bite out of her apple. "Dad'll get me one."

"Wasn't there some deal like all B's and A's on your report card first?" Christina teased.

Melanie waved her apple. "He's probably forgotten all about that."

Christina shook her head, still laughing. "You're dreaming, Mel. Hey, thanks for offering to help. I needed cheering up."

Melanie nodded. "You seemed pretty down at school. Is there something else bothering you?"

Stopping in the tack room, Christina picked up Star's grooming box and got the antibiotic from the refrigerator. Melanie pulled Star's halter and lead line from their peg on the wall.

"Well, it's about Star," Christina said as she went into the aisle. "I wasn't quite truthful at school. He *is* getting better, but . . ." She hesitated.

"But what?"

"I'll let you see for yourself. It might be my imagination."

Melanie followed Christina, her stomach tightening. Was Star getting worse? Was that what Christina was hinting at?

When they reached the stall, Christina swung open the door. Melanie stepped into the doorway, expecting the worst, but Star actually looked better. His ribs and hip bones still stuck out, but he wasn't quite so skeletal-looking, and his coat looked a little less dull.

Melanie gave Christina a questioning look.

"Just watch," Christina whispered. "Hey, handsome." Holding out her hand, Christina approached Star. He cocked one ear back, looked suspiciously at Christina, then moved away from her to the other side of the stall. Melanie was shocked. Star loved Christina. Why was he acting like that?

She glanced at Christina. Her cousin was blinking back tears.

"What's going on?" Melanie asked, her voice low.

"I don't know," Christina wailed. "But if you see it, too, then something really is wrong."

"He's acting like he did when he was at Townsend Acres," Melanie said. "Angry and suspicious. But that's too weird, because he's *not* at Townsend Acres."

Then her gaze fell on the disposable syringe in Christina's hand. "Wait a minute. It's the shots! I bet whenever you come near him, he thinks you're going to give him a shot."

Christina inhaled sharply. "You're probably right! Why didn't I think of that?"

"Because you've been so tired and worn out lately, you can hardly think straight." Melanie took the syringe from her and dropped it into the grooming bucket. "Let Ian or Maureen give him his shots from now on," Melanie said. "Star depends upon you for other things. You need to bring him carrots, not poke needles in his neck."

"That makes sense," Christina said, sounding relieved. "I've just been so intent on doing *everything* for him. Before, he didn't seem to pay any attention to the shots. But now he jumps like they really hurt." This time Christina approached him with her half-eaten apple. Star swung his head around, saw the apple in her palm, and stepped closer to eat it. Christina laughed. "Thanks, Mel. You're a genius. Are you ready to try that acupressure now?"

"Sure, but then I need to ask you a favor, too. Tonight Fredericka's going to watch me trot Image around her track. Elizabeth will be there, but I'd rather have your help. It'll be the first time I've ridden Image for Fredericka, and it's *got* to go right."

Christina grinned. "I'd love to help. Besides, I want to see you ride Image myself."

Mike drove right up to Fredericka's barn, stopping behind a big horse van that Melanie didn't recognize.

"Is Fredericka getting a new horse?" Mike asked.

"She didn't say anything to me about it," Melanie answered.

"I'll come get you in an hour," Mike said when the girls climbed out. "We can pick up Chinese takeout on the way home."

"Great." Melanie and Christina waved goodbye. Then Melanie walked over to the van, a sudden shiver racing up her arms. "This reminds me of the night Image left," she told Christina ominously.

"Hey, guys," Elizabeth called as she came out of the barn carrying a lead line.

"What's going on?" Melanie asked. A heavyset driver wearing dark sunglasses had gotten out of the van and was lowering the ramp.

"Fredericka bought a new colt," Elizabeth said. "I think she paid a lot of money for him. A whole lot."

"What makes you think that?" Melanie asked.

"Because this morning when she told me about him, she was acting really weird. She kept saying, 'Now, Elizabeth, when you unload Court Jester, you be extra careful. He's my million-dollar baby.' She kept saying 'million-dollar.'" Elizabeth shook her head. "It's not like her."

"You want me to get him out?" the driver asked.

"No, I'll do it." Elizabeth started up the ramp. Melanie could just make out the horse inside the van, his black tail swishing.

A minute later Elizabeth led the colt down the ramp. Stepping out of the way, Melanie looked him over. He was a copper-colored bay with a black mane and tail, flashy white socks, and a white stripe. When he reached the ground, the colt twisted his head around, taking everything in. Elizabeth held tight to the lead.

"He is gorgeous," Christina breathed.

"Yeah, but gorgeous doesn't mean he's going to win races," Melanie said. "What's his breeding?" she asked Elizabeth as she followed her and the colt into the barn.

"That's weird, too," Elizabeth answered. Stopping in the aisle, the colt stared around nervously. Elizabeth stroked his neck. "I saw the papers and didn't recognize the sire or dam or any grandsires."

"Where'd he come from?" Christina asked.

"Fairleigh Farm."

Fairleigh Farm. Thomas Blakely's farm.

Alarms went off in Melanie's head. Immediately

she pictured Thomas Blakely handing Alexis the envelope at Keeneland. "Let me guess. Alexis told Fredericka that she just *had* to buy this colt, right?"

"Well, yeah. I'm pretty sure Alexis found the colt for her."

Christina gave Melanie a puzzled look. "What are you saying?"

Melanie shook her head. "I'm not sure. It's just that Fredericka has been buying a lot of expensive horses lately. But when I talk to her, she seems worried about money. If that's true, how'd she afford to buy this colt?"

"She sold Master Charles," Elizabeth said.

"Master Charles!" Melanie repeated, shocked. "But he's Townsend Mistress's last foal! She loves that colt. She named him after her husband."

Elizabeth smiled sadly. "I loved him, too. That's why I was so surprised when she agreed to sell him. I guess Mr. Townsend offered her a price she couldn't refuse."

Melanie frowned. "Brad bought him?"

Elizabeth nodded. A horse whinnied loudly, and Court Jester answered back. "Well, I'd better get him in a stall before something happens."

"We'd better get going, too. Fredericka said she'd be here soon." As Melanie followed Christina into the tack room, she wondered what Alexis was up to. Why had she pushed Fredericka into selling a colt she loved just to buy another one with unremarkable bloodlines?

The answer was lurking in her brain, Melanie knew, but just then she didn't have time to search for it. She handed Christina Image's saddle and bridle, then grabbed the grooming box.

Trotting up to the fence, Image greeted them with a whinny. "Hey, pretty girl," Melanie said, climbing over the top rail. She jumped down and gave the filly a hug.

Christina was impressed. "Wow, she sure is different than she was the last time I saw her."

"Come on in. You can help me groom her."

"Promise she won't attack?" Christina teased as she opened the gate. Working together, the two girls got Image cleaned and tacked up in no time. Then Christina boosted Melanie into the saddle.

Melanie touched her heels against Image's sides, and the filly moved calmly forward. Melanie made her walk, halt, back, and perform a figure eight. "She looks terrific!" Christina called.

Melanie had to agree—Image felt terrific under her, too. Melanie's heart began to pound as she squeezed the filly into a trot. Without a hitch, they circled the pasture, reversed, halted, and trotted off from a halt. It was almost too good to be true.

"She's got such beautiful gaits. You two should train for dressage," Christina said. "Forget about racing."

Melanie halted Image in front of Christina, who was sitting on the top rail of the fence. "*No way.*" Leaning down, she let her arms hang on both sides of Image's neck. "Racing is in our blood, right, Image?" She straightened. "Ready to try the track? I'd like to go around a few times before Fredericka gets here."

"Sure." Jumping down, Christina opened the gate.

As Image walked through, Melanie could feel the filly's muscles tense and her stride grow bouncier. It was the first time she had been ridden outside the paddock.

"I'm glad you're with me," Melanie admitted to her cousin. She was starting to feel nervous. What if Image acted up the minute she set foot on the track? "She's been so good, I don't think she'll try anything, but . . ."

"But you never know," Christina finished Melanie's thought.

Walking beside Image's head, Christina escorted horse and rider to the gate leading into Tall Oaks' small grass practice track. It was shaded with tall trees and was about half the size of Whitebrook's full-sized dirt track.

"This is cute," Christina said. "Like a racetrack for miniature horses."

"Let's hope Image likes it. If she blows up—" Melanie gave her head a hard shake. She had to push thoughts like that out of her mind.

151

When Image was through the gate, Christina stepped aside and Melanie steered the filly counterclockwise. Ears swiveling with excitement, Image strode around the track, her hooves skimming the grass as if she were floating.

She likes it! Melanie thought, her adrenaline pumping even though she was trying to stay calm. She was right about Image; she had always been right. Racing *was* in the filly's blood. It wouldn't be long before they would prove it to the world.

But first she had to prove it to Fredericka.

As they strode around the final bend, Melanie heard the roar of a tractor. Image was used to the noise, so Melanie didn't think too much of it. But then the tractor rattled out of the barn, pulling a brand-new manure spreader behind it. Who could be stupid enough to drive that noisy thing right at her while she was riding Image? Then she recognized the driver. It was Drew, whom Alexis had hired recently to do barn work. Drew was a hard worker, but he obviously didn't have a clue about horses.

As the tractor rumbled closer, Image froze. Drew steered it into the field beside the track, the spreader rattling and clanking behind it. Waving her arms, Christina hollered at Drew to stop, but he couldn't hear her over the noise of the motor. Snorting wildly, Image backed up, her whole body tensing for flight.

152

Don't be a hero. Just jump off, Melanie told herself. She could always get back on when Fredericka arrived.

Kicking her feet from the stirrups, Melanie was about to do an emergency dismount when Image suddenly reared high.

"Whoa," Melanie cried, desperately grasping the pommel. The spreader began to turn, and manure started flying everywhere, scaring Image even more.

"Whoa!" Melanie cried again as the filly landed on all fours. She wheeled, flinging Melanie sideways. Melanie grabbed mane, trying to keep her balance. But the filly reared again, her hooves striking the air as if she were fighting an enemy. Still holding the reins, Melanie slid backward. If she could just stay on!

Suddenly the reins snapped, and Melanie plummeted to the ground, landing hard on her shoulder. Image took off, the broken reins flying in the air.

Christina shut the gate and walked over to help Melanie up. Melanie got to her feet but remained silent, transfixed by the sight of Image. The filly was galloping around the track as if in a race. The tractor and spreader were still churning along, but Image didn't seem to care. Her neck was flat, her tail streaming behind her. It looked as though the filly was having a blast.

Melanie rubbed her shoulder. She didn't think she'd broken anything, but it hurt like crazy.

"I guess she's okay. I just wish that guy would stop making all that noise. Are you all right, Mel?" Christina asked, her face pale with worry.

Melanie nodded slowly. "I think so."

Christina didn't look convinced. "Try to move your arm."

Supporting her elbow with her right hand, Melanie rotated her left shoulder. "It's okay. Just banged up." Tears came into her eyes. "Don't worry," she said quickly when Christina furrowed her brow. "I'm not crying because of my shoulder. It's Image. I can't believe she acted so crazy. She was doing so well!"

Christina smiled cheerfully. "Don't be so hard on yourself. That spreader would have spooked any horse."

"It's not just that, Chris." Melanie shook her head, flooded with doubt. "Whenever I start feeling confident about Image and her training, something like this happens. What if Fredericka had been here? What if she'd seen me get dumped?" Melanie swallowed a sob of misery. "That would have been it for us. Maybe everybody's right. Maybe Image *is* bad luck, and I'm just wasting my time!"

11

"MELANIE, YOU'RE *NOT* WASTING YOUR TIME," CHRISTINA said, and touched Melanie's arm. "I know exactly how you're feeling right now, believe me. Star takes one step forward, then two steps back. It's really, really hard to believe he'll get better. But Mel, I won't *ever* give up on Star. And you shouldn't give up on Image, either. You love her as much as I love Star. Besides"— she gave Melanie a wicked smile—"Fredericka *wasn't* here. And *I'll* never tell her you fell off."

Melanie choked out a laugh. "Thanks, Chris."

"Feel better?"

Nodding, Melanie wiped her eyes and mustered a smile. "Yeah, and you're right. Image has done so well this past week. That's the important thing. I don't know what I'm doing standing here crying—I'd better catch her!"

The girls watched Image gallop around the far turn of the grass track, her hooves barely skimming the turf. "I wish I had a stopwatch," Melanie breathed. "She's flying."

"Yeah, it reminds me of the time she got loose and raced Gratis around Turfway."

Melanie grimaced. "See what I mean? Every time she gets on a track, she goes nuts."

"But look how in control she is. That's not nuts, Mel," Christina pointed out. "That's speed."

Christina was right. Silently Melanie counted off seconds in her head. If she was anywhere near close, Image had run five furlongs in under fifty-eight seconds.

Melanie's pulse quickened. That *was* fast.

When Image came down the homestretch Melanie stepped into the middle of the track. "Whoa, Image," she commanded. "Whoa."

The filly slowed to a canter, then a trot. She passed Melanie, circled, then trotted back, tossing her head as if to say, *Wasn't that fun?*

Melanie grabbed the dangling reins. "Come here, you bad girl. What if you had stepped on the reins? You could have fallen and broken your neck."

She ran her hand down the filly's heaving chest. Stooping, she checked her front legs.

"Is she all right?" Christina asked.

"Yeah. She's barely breathing hard. And look at her!" Neck arched, Image was gazing around triumphantly, as if she had just won a race.

"The look of a champion," Christina remarked admiringly.

Melanie snorted. "The look of a spoiled brat. I hate to let her get away with this kind of behavior."

Christina held up the lead line. "You know what you have to do. You can use this in place of the broken rein."

"I can't believe the rein broke, on top of everything else. It snapped so easily." Melanie studied the frayed ends where the rein had broken. In one spot the leather looked ragged, as if it had been pulled apart. The rest of the break looked as if the leather had been sliced clean through with a knife. "Look at this." She held out the ends. "Someone cut it."

"What?" Christina checked it over. "Wow. I think you might be right. But who would do that? You could have gotten seriously hurt."

Melanie scowled. "Good question, but I think I know. Do me a favor. Walk Image a minute while I talk to Drew."

Christina hooked the lead to Image's bit. Melanie jogged over to the field where Drew was spreading the manure.

When he steered the tractor closer, Melanie waved

her arm to catch his attention. "Hey, Drew," she called when he glanced her way. "Thanks for scaring my horse half to death."

"Huh?" Drew gave her a puzzled look.

"You scared my horse!" Melanie clarified. "Didn't you see me fall off?"

"I'm sorry. But Alexis told me to spread this load on the field."

Alexis. What a surprise.

Melanie remembered how Alexis had turned the colts into the field beside Image when she'd been working her on the longe lines. She was sure the farm manager had done that on purpose. And now this. Alexis must have known Fredericka was coming to watch her. Had she cut the rein to make sure Melanie would have an accident, just in case the noise Drew made with the spreader wasn't enough? But why would Alexis do something so stupid and dangerous?

Melanie was determined to find out. Jaw clenched, she jogged up to the barn. She could hear Alexis talking in the office. Dropping to a walk, Melanie went slowly down the aisle. As she neared the office she could hear Alexis more clearly.

"Don't worry, Brad, it's working. Fredericka will be calling to accept your offer within the next few days, and Melanie will be out of our hair."

So Alexis is *up to something with Brad*, Melanie

158

thought angrily. She had been right all along. Furious, Melanie stepped into the office, stopping in the doorway. Alexis's brows shot up when she saw her, but she continued talking into the phone as if nothing were wrong.

"Great, Mr. Townsend, I'll tell Fredericka how pleased you are with Master Charles. And thank you," she said in a businesslike tone. She hung up and swiveled to face Melanie. "Hi. What can I do for you?" Alexis's voice was smooth as silk.

Melanie was amazed. Alexis was such a polished liar, Melanie had no doubt she'd done this type of thing before.

"You know, Alexis," Melanie began, keeping her voice equally smooth, "you're beautiful, smart, and an excellent farm manager. But you're also a nasty control freak, and I know you've been scamming Fredericka."

Fixing a cool eye on Melanie, Alexis folded her arms across her chest. "You're the one scamming Fredericka. You keep convincing her to pour time and money into that crazy horse. I saw her dump you and race around the track like an idiot. It's a wonder you weren't hurt."

"The only reason I fell is because the rein broke. And the reason it broke is because it was cut."

"Oh, so you're trying to blame me for your little mishap? Sorry, that's not going to work. Fredericka

159

should be here any minute with Vince, and believe me, I'm going to tell her what happened. By the time I'm finished, she'll wish she'd sold Image ages ago. Brad certainly offered her good money."

"If Image is so crazy, why would you want Brad to have her? You seem to have such a great relationship with him." Suddenly it dawned on Melanie what Alexis had been up to. "Wait a minute. That's how you know how much Brad offered Fredericka. That's why you want her to sell Image to Brad. You're getting money from him, aren't you?"

Alexis shrugged. "Brad offered me a broker's fee. Nothing illegal in that."

"I'm not sure Fredericka would see it that way," Melanie snapped. "How many horses have you bought and sold for her? Six?" Melanie tallied up the figures in her head. "Let's say you've been getting fifteen percent, which is standard. That means you made a hundred fifty thousand dollars on Court Jester—that is, if he really cost a million dollars. I bet that's what was in the envelope Thomas Blakely handed you. Then you made about seventy-five thousand on Master Charles. No wonder you were so eager to sell Charles to Brad and have Fredericka buy Jester, who's probably not even as well bred. You made a load of money on both sales." Melanie narrowed her eyes, studying Alexis. The farm manager had a hard look on her face, and suddenly

Melanie didn't think she was pretty at all.

"And that's only two horses," Melanie continued, getting angrier the more she thought about what Alexis had been doing to Fredericka. "I can't imagine how much you made off her stallion, Khan, and Gratis. In fact, I bet you've made a *pile* of money since you've been working at Tall Oaks. You probably don't need to work much longer. You can retire!"

"So what's your point?" Alexis didn't even look rattled. "It's not illegal, you have no proof that I've done anything wrong, and Fredericka has agreed with every sale or purchase. In fact, she's delighted with the horses she's bought."

"Only because she trusts you. She thinks you're doing this for *her*."

"I *am* doing this for her." Alexis waved her hand in the direction of the new stallion wing. "Khan's booked solid for next year's breeding season, and look how much purse money Gratis has won for her."

"Except now she's buying horses she can't afford," Melanie pointed out. "And selling horses she loves based on *your* recommendation. If she keeps it up, she'll go broke while you get rich. You'd probably like that, wouldn't you? Then you could get a big fat commission on the closeout sale."

"Wow. You sure have a vivid imagination," Alexis said, rolling her eyes.

161

"Maybe. But what happens when I tell Fredericka that you pick horses to buy and sell based on how much money you'll make, when you should be buying horses that will improve her racing or breeding program?"

Alexis snorted. "Go ahead and tell her. Why should she believe you?"

"I'm sure the owners and dealers who paid you the broker's fees will be happy to talk to Fredericka."

"You're so naive, Melanie." Alexis smirked. "Don't you think they made money on the deals, too?"

Melanie's jaw tightened. "Okay. But you're not going to get your way with Image. I heard what you said to Brad on the phone, and you're wrong. Your plan is not working. Image behaved herself and ran around the track like a champ."

Alexis's expression was stony. "You're the only one who thinks she'll amount to anything."

"Fredericka does, too."

"Not after I fill her in on what just happened."

This time it was Melanie's turn to smirk. "Go ahead. But when I tell her what you've been doing, I don't think she's going to listen to you anymore. Tomorrow Image is going to Whitebrook, where she'll get trained as a racehorse." Reaching down, Melanie picked up the phone receiver and held it out. "Why don't you call Brad and give him that message?"

"I don't think so." Alexis yanked the receiver from Melanie's grasp and plunked it down. "You haven't won yet, Melanie."

"I think I have," Melanie said. "Fredericka may not believe me when I tell her my suspicions about you, but the next time you want her to buy or sell a horse, she's going to think twice." Melanie gave Alexis her cockiest New York smile, and for the first time she saw a flicker of doubt in the farm manager's eyes. "Your scam is over, Alexis."

With that, Melanie hurried from the barn. As she jogged down to the track, she felt as though a huge weight had been lifted from her shoulders. For the first time she felt sure of herself and of Image.

Image *wasn't* bad luck. She wasn't perfect, either, but Melanie suspected that Alexis had been behind many of Image's mishaps. She'd always wondered about the possibility, but it had never made sense. Now she knew she was right, and she knew the reason why.

Greed.

As she jogged down the hill, Melanie's heart felt light. Christina was walking beside Image, talking to her. The filly's ears were cocked, as if she was listening. She swung her head around to look at Melanie and whinnied loudly.

"What happened?" Christina asked as she led Image toward the gate.

"I'll tell you later." Stopping, Melanie caught her breath. "I want to get back in the saddle. Will you give me a leg up? Fredericka should be here any minute. Vince is going to be with her. I want to make sure they see Image trotting around the track."

Christina cupped a hand around Melanie's knee and boosted her into the saddle, then gave her the lead line to use as a rein. Again Melanie felt as if her head were in the clouds—in more ways than one. She was dizzy with hope that Fredericka and Vince would finally see Image as the racehorse she was born to be.

Anxious, she adjusted the girth and fiddled with her helmet strap, the whole time keeping her eye on the barn. Alexis had said they'd be here any minute. It was way after five-thirty. "Where are they?" Melanie fretted out loud.

"Quit worrying. I'll go find Fredericka and make sure she sees you. Good luck." Stepping away, Christina added, "You okay?"

"Nervous but okay." Taking a deep breath, Melanie squeezed her heels against Image's sides. The filly strode off eagerly. Drew had finished spreading manure, and the fields were quiet. Christina was striding up the hill toward the barn. The sun was setting, a cool breeze wafted against Melanie's cheek, and a whippoorwill sang in the distance.

Melanie clucked, and Image broke into a jog, then a

canter. It was the first time Melanie had ever cantered the filly, and for an instant she panicked. Sitting deep in the saddle, she started to pull back on the reins. But then she felt the soft, steady rhythm of Image's gait and knew it would be okay. Fredericka had asked for only a jog, but seeing Image breeze easily around the track would take her breath away. Tilting her body forward, Melanie balanced her weight on her heels. As they cantered around the first bend, Image seemed to float beneath her.

From the corner of her eye she spotted Vince, Fredericka, and Christina coming out of the barn. "This is it, girl," Melanie whispered. "Let's show them what you've got."

Image flicked her ears and lengthened her stride, as if she understood. As they breezed around the track, power radiated through Image, as if she'd been doing this all her life. Her hooves beat against the earth in time with the beat of Melanie's heart.

Tears of joy filled Melanie's eyes. *This* was what she'd been working for!

She glanced toward the barn. Vince, Christina, and Fredericka were standing in front of the open doors, watching. Vince had his arms crossed over his chest. The brim of his fedora hid his expression. But Fredericka waved a handkerchief, then pressed it against her mouth as if she was going to cry with joy.

Melanie knew exactly how she felt.

• • •

Tuesday morning Melanie woke up early, too excited to sleep. Image was coming to Whitebrook! Jumping out of bed, she padded into Christina's bedroom. Her cousin's head was buried under her pillow "Wake up, sleepyhead!" Melanie sang out.

"Go away," Christina mumbled grumpily.

"I can't. I need someone to talk to. I'm about to burst."

"Go down to the barn," Christina's words were muffled. "You can talk to the horses. And tell those birds outside my window to stop singing. We don't have to be at school for—" She peeked at the clock from under the pillow. "Five hours?"

Melanie laughed. "There aren't any birds singing. It's too early even for them." She patted the pillow, which Christina had retreated under. "Don't sleep much longer. Image should be here in about two hours. Joe's bringing her on his way from Keeneland. What if I make a batch of blueberry muffins? Would that get you out of bed?"

A muffled grunt told Melanie she should give up on Christina. Humming, she hurried downstairs, taking the steps by twos. Ashleigh was already in the kitchen, making a pot of coffee. She was in her bathrobe, her brown hair tousled. "Excited?" she asked.

Melanie nodded. "Too excited to sleep. Mind if I make some breakfast?"

"Sounds great. I'm starving. Mike should be in from the barn any minute. He's going over the morning works with Cindy. And the vet is coming soon to look at Catwink."

"Is something wrong with Catwink? Is that why Joe's bringing her back from the track?"

"She's favoring her left foreleg. But there's no heat and it's not puffy. We'll probably have to do an ultrasound."

Banging through the cupboards, Melanie got out flour, sugar, and muffin tins. Ashleigh sat in the kitchen chair, sipping her coffee. "Melanie, now that Image will be here at Whitebrook and you'll be around more, we'd like you to exercise horses for us again in the mornings. And we want you to jockey for us, starting this Saturday."

When Ashleigh mentioned jockeying, Melanie felt a rush of excitement. "Do you mean it, Aunt Ashleigh? I feel like I'm completely out of practice."

"Of course we mean it. We've missed you around here. And don't forget about your win on Raven. Mel, you're one of our best riders."

"Thanks. I'd love to get back to racing. But I want to make sure I give Image as much attention as I can. She's already behind all the other fillies her age. I want to put her in a race as soon as possible."

Ashleigh paused between sips. "Just don't rush her," she warned. "I know Fredericka was really pleased after seeing you ride her yesterday, but that's a long way from breezing on a real track, in a field of horses, in a real race."

"I know. But even Vince was impressed." Melanie laughed. "Well, he didn't say he was impressed, but he didn't snarl and growl as much as he usually does."

"Then he must have been impressed." Ashleigh laughed with her.

Impulsively Melanie ran over and hugged her aunt around the shoulders, smudging flour on her robe. "Thank you, Aunt Ashleigh, for believing in me," Melanie said, her throat tight with emotion and her voice thick. "Thank you for letting Image come to Whitebrook. Thank you for everything!"

"You're welcome, Melanie," Ashleigh replied, sounding just as moved.

Turning abruptly, Melanie tried to concentrate on making the muffins, but every noise made her run to the window to see if Joe was pulling up to the barn.

It wasn't until almost seven o'clock, when Melanie and Christina were cleaning up after breakfast, that the van finally arrived. Dropping the muffin tin she was drying, Melanie raced out the door with Christina right behind her. By the time they reached the training barn, Joe was parking the van and a crowd was beginning to gather. Mike, Cindy, Ashleigh, and Ian came from the barn to watch. Even Kevin hobbled over, his knee still wrapped in a bandage.

Melanie heard a loud bang from inside the van as one of the horses kicked the stall wall.

"I couldn't stand going to school until I found out whether Image lived up to her bad-girl reputation and tore down the van door," Kevin joked.

"Don't even start," Melanie warned.

"That's Catwink," Joe said when he swung from the cab of the van. "She's been doing that all the way from Keeneland. Image and Pirate have been quiet as lambs."

"How did they load?" Mike asked. "We were wondering what took you so long."

"They loaded fine. Thank goodness, because I didn't have any help. Fredericka was the only one at Tall Oaks."

"Where was Alexis?" Melanie asked.

Joe shrugged. "Fredericka said she quit. Walked out without any warning."

Melanie's brows shot up and she glanced at Christina, who didn't look at all surprised. The day before, Melanie had been prepared to tell Fredericka all about Alexis. But Fredericka had been so elated to see Image cantering around the track that she'd announced that the filly was definitely ready for Whitebrook. When Vince agreed, Melanie had been too thrilled to break the bad news. And if Alexis had quit, she didn't think she needed to. Fredericka would figure things out for herself.

"Maybe she went back to California," Ian said. "I heard rumors she was taking advantage of Fredericka and that Vince was going to do something about it."

"Who told you that?" Melanie asked.

Ian shrugged. "I hear things," he said, and everybody laughed.

"If Alexis quit, Fredericka's going to have to hire a new farm manager," Cindy said.

When everybody swung around to look at her, she held up her hand. "Don't look at me. I'm going to be too busy recuperating from my operation."

"You decided to have it?" Melanie asked.

Reluctantly Cindy smiled. "Let's just say I was talked into it," she said, looking sideways at Ian, who was pretending he hadn't heard what his daughter had said.

"Will you take Pirate?" Melanie asked Kevin, handing him an extra lead. "We're putting the two of them together in the big paddock by the drive."

Melanie helped Joe unlatch the heavy ramp and lower it to the ground. When she spotted Image's beautiful dished face, her eyes filled with tears.

She hurried up the ramp, with Kevin following right after her. Image greeted her with a soft nicker. "Hey, pretty girl." Melanie stroked her neck. "How was the ride?"

Image bobbed her head, jingling the chains hooked to her halter rings

"You're as excited as I am, aren't you?" Melanie asked. Undoing the chains, she snapped on the lead line. Next to her, Kevin was waiting to lead Pirate out. Beside Pirate, Catwink pawed the van floor impatiently.

Melanie took a deep breath. This was it—the beginning of a whole new chapter in Image's life. Melanie knew it wasn't going to be easy, but she was more than ready for the challenge. Clucking, she steered the filly from the narrow stall. Image halted at the top of the ramp, her dark eyes wide and curious as she took in her new surroundings.

"Take a good look, Perfect Image," Melanie said, her heart bursting with pride. "This is Whitebrook, the best horse farm in the whole world, and I know you're going to love it here as much as I do!"

ALICE LEONHARDT has been horse-crazy since she was five years old. Her first pony was a pinto named Ted. When she got older, she joined Pony Club and rode in shows and rallies. Now she just rides her quarter horse, April, for fun. The author of more than thirty books for children, she still finds time to take care of two horses, two cats, two dogs, and two children, as well as teach at a community college.